His pas *her breathless*

"Lucas..." That sounded soft, trembling, feminine...no way to deal with his gentle forcefulness. "All I want is to be left alone!"

"And do you always get what you want, Victoria?"

She drew a deep breath and felt his fingertips against her lower ribs, his palms cupping her sides, felt his strength and warmth and vibrant life flowing into her, spreading through her cold body, melting her resistance. Lean on me, he seemed to be saying. But she couldn't.

"It's bad for people to get what they want all the time...." she said harshly.

"There speaks the vicar's daughter. Do you know what I want?"

Her imagination running rampant, she shook her head dumbly, and he smiled, a sexy quirk of his uneven mouth....

SUSAN NAPIER was born on Valentine's Day, so perhaps it is only fitting that she should become a romance writer. She started out as a reporter for New Zealand's largest evening newspaper before resigning to marry the paper's chief reporter. After the birth of their two children she did some free-lancing for a film-production company and then settled down to write her first romance. "Now," she says, "I am in the enviable position of being able to build my career around my home and family."

Books by Susan Napier

HARLEQUIN PRESENTS
1252—THE LOVE CONSPIRACY
1284—A BEWITCHING COMPULSION
1332—FORTUNE'S MISTRESS
1380—NO REPRIEVE
1460—DEAL OF A LIFETIME
1483—DEVIL TO PAY

HARLEQUIN ROMANCE
2711—LOVE IN THE VALLEY
2723—SWEET VIXEN

Don't miss any of our special offers. Write to us at the following address for information on our newest releases.

Harlequin Reader Service
P.O. Box 1397, Buffalo, NY 14240
Canadian address: P.O. Box 603,
Fort Erie, Ont. L2A 5X3

SUSAN NAPIER

Tempt Me Not

Harlequin Books

TORONTO • NEW YORK • LONDON
AMSTERDAM • PARIS • SYDNEY • HAMBURG
STOCKHOLM • ATHENS • TOKYO • MILAN
MADRID • WARSAW • BUDAPEST • AUCKLAND

Love is a driver, bitter and fierce if you fight
and resist him,
Easygoing enough once you acknowledge his
power.

Ovid

Harlequin Presents first edition February 1993
ISBN 0-373-11531-8

Original hardcover edition published in 1991
by Mills & Boon Limited

TEMPT ME NOT

CHAPTER ONE

'SORRY, miss. No invite, no entry.'

Victoria West stared in frustration at the man who had just listened to her plight with every evidence of sincere sympathy. 'I'm not a miss,' she said firmly.

'What?' The stocky, bull-headed young man looked impatiently over her head at the group of shadows hanging around the open gates at the end of the driveway. People had been overlooking Victoria for most of her twenty-five years, but tonight she couldn't afford to enjoy her comfortable obscurity. Tonight was important to David, and for his sake she couldn't let herself be casually turned away. She was already embarrassingly late, thanks to the wretched car.

Victoria brandished her wedding-ring, hoping it would convince him that she was a mature, respectable member of society and not one of those potentially troublesome shadows from the gate.

He shrugged, unimpressed. 'Still not an invitation, ma'am. Now, if you wouldn't mind stepping aside...'

More late arrivals, but these didn't appear to share her anxiety about their tardiness. How Victoria wished she could emulate their confidence. The two couples breezed past her as if she didn't exist, chattering and laughing as they handed their gold-edged cards to the doorman. In trying to give them room Victoria stumbled off the edge of the brick-paved path right into the clutches of a rambling rose. She pricked her fingers trying to free her ankles from the fragrant but unloving embrace.

Victoria battled a fatalistic sense of defeat. It just wasn't her night. Forgetting to bring her invitation had been out of character—she was normally very conscientious—but her nerves had got the better of her. She had

7

been ready hours before time and yet still managed to be in a frantic rush at the last minute. She was definitely not a party animal and David knew it. That was why, when he had called earlier to amend their plans, asking her to meet him at the Greys' house rather than wait for him to pick her up, he had taken pains to reassure her that the evening was to be a 'small and select' dinner party. Evidently David's idea of small and select was not her own. From the long list in the security man's hand and the number of cars parked in the street, 'select' appeared to mean half of Auckland city! Apart from anything else, if Victoria had to go back to her car, which was parked some distance away, she would have to run the gauntlet of those slightly scary young people hanging around the gate. She decided that abasing herself was the lesser evil.

'Perhaps if I could speak to Miss Grey——' she begged bravely.

'Is she a friend of yours?'

'Well, no,' confessed Victoria with scrupulous honesty, 'we've never met, but my—Mr West—David West, that is—has . . . is . . . I mean, he works for Mr Grey——'

She was so flustered that the truth was coming out as awkwardly as a lie. Since for some reason David's name wasn't on the guest-list, she could hardly blame the man for his disbelief. After all, it was his job to resist bribery, blandishments and menace with equal loyalty.

'Do I look like a gatecrasher? Or a thief?' she asked in desperation.

The greatest compliment that Victoria considered she had ever had was being told that she had an open face. Even the security-man relented in his grimness and grinned a little as he looked down from the twin vantage points of his considerable height and the steps between them. Who could be afraid of Victoria? Although she was of medium height she somehow gave the impression of being smaller. In the night shadows her gentle eyes were a dark, indeterminate colour and so was her shoulder-length brown hair, untidily ruffled from her battle with the stubborn spare tyre. She liked to tell herself that she had a face with character but she knew that the soft oval contained too little definition. Even her nose was neatly nondescript. The crowning touch on the picture of innocent non-aggression was the mass of pale ginger freckles that smothered her creamy skin from head to foot. Victoria had a redhead's skin but unfortunately not a redhead's dramatic colouring to redress the balance.

'Sorry—more than my job's worth...' This time he sounded as if he actually meant it. Victoria stiffened. She didn't like being pitied, but if it meant getting into the house... She hesitantly mounted a step, giving him her best, most waiflike smile of pleading.

'Look, I——'

'Problem?'

A man passing the lighted hallway behind the formally dressed security guard paused in silhouette to utter the clipped enquiry.

'Uh, no, not really.' The guard was suddenly all deference. 'This young woman says she's left her invitation behind. Says that she's supposed to be with a David West, but he's not on my guest-list either——'

'He wouldn't be, since he's helping to host, but he hasn't arrived yet,' murmured the man after a brief hesitation, stepping over the threshold to extend a hand to Victoria. A faint Canadian burr was the only hint of his early origins. 'I'm Lucas Grey.'

So this was David's boss—the electronics genius he was always singing praises about. Victoria put her small hand in his, her own introduction stalling in her throat as she looked up...and up...at him. An intellectual giant indeed! Through her husband she had met a number of acclaimed geniuses and had noticed a collective similarity, an intellectual other-worldliness, that generally rendered them physically unintimidating. In fact, given their remoteness from the material world and their often careless attitude to their appearance, health and manners, most of them had succeeded in triggering her maternal instincts rather than any sense of inferiority.

Lucas Grey didn't conform to that reassuring pattern
at all. He was big, very big. Even the beautifully tailored
dinner-jacket couldn't disguise the muscled strength that
padded his shoulders and chest. His face, as the exterior
light fell on it, was hard and handsome, full of very
sharply defined planes and angles unsoftened by the coal-
black hair and the thick brows and lashes framing his
dark eyes. Victoria couldn't help looking at his mouth
as he stopped speaking. In repose it was fascinatingly
uneven. A very sexy, cynical mouth. In fact the man was
'very' everything. The unexpected waywardness of her
thoughts horrified her and she tried to withdraw her
hand, but suddenly he stiffened and applied a swift
counterforce, pulling her forward into the spotlight with
him.

The politely curious expression of welcome on the hard
face vanished. His black eyes narrowed as they shafted
over her face and dipped to linger on the small gold and
emerald pendant that lay against her cream silk blouse.
When they lifted again they were grim with inexplicable
anger. His hand tightened on hers, so painfully that she
gasped. He held the pressure a brief, deliberate moment
longer and then released her crushed hand and turned
his broad back on her. He said something in an undertone to the guard, who was obviously startled, because
it had to be tersely repeated. Then, to Victoria's shock,
Lucas Grey walked back into the house without another
glance.

It was left to the guard to enlighten her and this time
he seemed as embarrassed as she.

'Uh—I'm sorry, miss—uh, ma'am—Mr Grey says—
well, I'm afraid I'll have to ask you to leave the premises.'

'But—I was *invited*. You heard him say that Mr West
was helping to host——'

Even as she protested she knew it was no use trying
to get the man to disobey his employer. Lucas Grey did
more than conform to the pattern, he *redefined* it—he
was the rudest man she had ever met! The body of a
bull and the manners to match, she told herself dis-
gustedly as she walked back down the driveway. Even

if meeting her had triggered some complex theorem in his brain that required his immediate and full attention, that was no excuse for leaving her high and dry. Well, at least she could tell David that she had tried...

'Tory, what are you doing? You're not looking at the gardens at this time of night?'

'David!' She was so glad to see him that she didn't take him to task for the ridiculous question. He knew she loved pottering around in her garden, but she wasn't a fanatic.

He slid an arm around her and reversed her progress on the path. 'Sorry I'm so late, but I got held up at the office. I really did intend to be here before you but... well... this has been one hell of a day!'

As they passed one of the downlights illuminating the rose-bushes Victoria got a glimpse of his face. Tall and athletic, with tanned skin and sun-bleached blond hair, David always looked the picture of health, and the formal dinner-wear suited him. In the nine years she had known him he had seemed to grow more good-looking every year. When she had met him off the plane that afternoon from a week-long business trip to Sydney, and driven him direct to his office, he had seemed in a particularly buoyant mood, but tonight there was a pinched look around his mouth and he looked much more than his youthful twenty-six.

'What happened?' she asked gently. David had just been promoted to the corporate public relations division of Computel Industries and Victoria knew that, although he was confident of his abilities, he was still somewhat tentative in his new position.

He shrugged tiredly. 'I haven't worked it out yet...but I will. You haven't been waiting out here for me all this time, have you?'

Victoria took the hint. She loved him and they were very close, but she respected his privacy. If only he would respect hers just as much!

'I've only just arrived myself,' she confessed guiltily.

'This late? What happened?' His instant concern took his mind off his own worries. 'I didn't see Jason. Don't tell me he just dropped you off at the gate?'

'Jason had gone out by the time you called. I drove myself over.'

'Why didn't you say something?' he demanded. 'I would have come and picked you up if I'd known——'

'I know, and then you would have been even later than you are,' Victoria pointed out softly. 'I'm a perfectly good driver, David, and after all it was only a few streets. If I hadn't had a—forgotten the invitation,' she edited herself hurriedly, 'I'd have been inside by now...'

'Surely you didn't bother to trek back for it?'

'I was just going to. The security man on the door wouldn't let me in,' she admitted ruefully.

'Well, they do have to be careful, you know,' said David soothingly. 'This place is stuffed with valuable art. You should have asked for Lucas and told him who you were.'

'I didn't have the chance. He came to the door, heard I was with you, and told the security guard to throw me out.'

'He didn't!' David stopped in his tracks, looking stricken. 'Oh, God, she must have told him! I can't believe this is happening——' The lines of tension set in his face. 'She can't do this to me——'

'Who?'

'Gabby—Gabrielle. We had one hell of a yelling match this afternoon when she came into the office and then she took off and this crisis blew up and I had to stay behind... The whole thing is completely ridiculous! I thought she might have calmed down by now. Tonight was supposed to be——' He broke off and muttered under his breath. 'Well, if she thinks her paranoia is going to lose me my job or let her insult you she's got another think coming. Come on.'

With that grim pronouncement he planted a firm hand in the small of Victoria's back and propelled her towards the steps she had trailed ignominiously down a few minutes before.

'David, won't you please tell me what's going on?' Victoria knew that David and Gabrielle Grey, Lucas's sister and co-owner of Computel, were working closely together on a new project, but she also knew that easy-going David rarely lost his temper.

'Sure. When I find out myself. My name is David West,' he told the security man, looking him straight in the eye. 'This lady is with me, and she's coming in. If Mr Grey wants us to leave we will, quietly, with no trouble. But I'm going to see him first.'

The security man gave him a shrewd measuring look and nodded but as they moved into the stark white foyer David gave an exclamation of horror.

'Tory!'

'What?' She looked down at herself and groaned. The ankles of her black glitter tights had several tiny holes, three of which had run halfway up her shins. Her very best, most glamorous pair of stockings sabotaged by vicious flowers! If she had been wearing a long dress the damage would still have been noticeable, but displayed by the knee-length flounced black silk taffeta it was glaringly obvious.

'Oh, David, I can't go in there like this!' She waved a distraught hand towards the clink-and-buzz of social conversation further down the hall. 'I'll have to go home.'

'We can't. Not until I've seen Gabby.' David's mouth twisted wryly. 'I hope you shaved your legs today, Tory.'

'Wha——?'

'Come on.' He ducked into a nearby room and flipped the light-switch as he shut the door. The room was as starkly white as the hall, and had obviously just been redecorated. The smell was quite strong and there was a sealed can of white paint sitting on a drop cloth under the bare window. The thick grey carpet was fluffing under their feet, attesting to its newness. The only fur-niture was a huge black leather chair, with protective cloths still tucked under its castors, although there were a few black and white Picasso prints already hung around the walls, Victoria realised as David shunted her towards the chair.

'Hurry up,' David urged impatiently, sliding a hand up her thigh. 'Let's get 'em off and see what you look like!'

'David!' Victoria slapped his hand away and put her black velvet evening bag down on the couch so she could tackle the task. David grinned, lightening the harassed expression on his face.

'You should feel privileged. Do you know, you're the only woman in the world that I feel I can be completely natural with. I wonder why that is.'

'Because I'm safe; you don't have to impress me in order for me to love you.' Surprisingly, in spite of his outgoing nature, and frequent well-meaning advice from his two younger sisters, David had always been a little awkward and fumbling in his relationships with women. Privately Victoria thought it was because of his looks. The girls had started to chase him before he was old enough to cope with the unwelcome attention and he had reacted by developing a defensive shyness that had unfortunately become an ingrained habit in the fully grown man.

'But I do. I've always wanted to live up to your expectations for me ... I suppose because you never tried to thrust them on me the way other people generally do. I think it's a matter of trust. You're such a loving, giving person. I can't imagine you ever hurting anyone, deliberately or otherwise. You always manage to make things seem ... better; to get people to see the possibilities instead of just the pessimistic probabilities. Just having you here is like having a good-luck charm with me ...'

'I hope *I* can live up to *your* expectations,' joked Victoria, going pink at his flattery as she struggled out of the tights and slipped her feet back into the black shoes with little cream bows on the heels. 'There, how do I look?' She felt awfully naked without stockings, even though in the late summer warmth of March they really weren't necessary, but she couldn't say that to David after his slew of compliments!

They both looked down at her cream-and-freckle legs and then at each other. They exchanged weak smiles.

'I suppose I'll have my legs under the table most of the time anyway,' said Victoria comfortingly. 'Providing we're allowed to stay to dinner, of course...'

She was sorry she had reminded him of his troubles when his smile was swallowed by a frown.

'I wanted this to go so well, this meeting between you and the Greys. I wanted it to be nice and informal——'

'Informal?' Victoria was incredulous. 'In evening clothes, at a dinner party this size...'

'...when you hate parties, I know, I know,' said David glumly. 'But I figured you'd find it more comfortable this way, in a crowd, rather than having all their attention focused on you...'

Victoria could appreciate his logic, twisted though it was. It was true, you could hide in a crowd. In a one-to-one meeting, her tongue-tiedness with strangers would be excruciatingly obvious.

'I mean, you've always refused to come to any of the Computel functions with me. But I thought it was long past time that Gabby and Lucas met my family...' He tailed off when he saw the dawning comprehension in Victoria's dark green eyes. 'I love her; I have for ages but I only realised it last week.' He hesitated, then blurted out, 'I've asked her to marry me.'

'And she turned you down? Oh, David, I'm sorry!' Victoria put consoling arms around him. She knew that David had liked Gabrielle Grey—he had talked about her often—but, reserved as he was with women, she had never suspected the depth of his feelings. No wonder he had been behaving oddly of late.

'No. That's the point!' he said wretchedly, moving impatiently away to pace up and down. 'She said she loved me too, but that she didn't want to rush into anything just yet. Then she turned up in Sydney on Monday and we...I...well, she didn't actually *say* she'd marry me, but naturally after we...' He went bright red at Victoria's gentle smile and stumbled thickly on. 'It was so fantastic that I naturally assumed——! Tory, she gave me every reason to believe that saying yes was only a formality! We even looked at rings at the same place I got that pendant for you and she said she was looking forward to meeting you. And then I get back today and she blows up at me. Practically accused me of running a harem! *Me?*'

He was right to sound incredulous. Victoria could count on one hand the number of serious girlfriends he'd had since he left school. In the last eight months with Computel he hadn't had a single date, other than outings with his colleagues. Victoria had naïvely assumed that it was because he found his work so completely absorbing and satisfying.

'I'm sure if you talk to her you'll be able to straighten this little misunderstanding out,' she soothed. 'These things happen when you're in love.'

'I don't remember you and Josh ever fighting about anything.'

'Well, no, but we were different.' Victoria smiled wryly. 'We had our disagreements, but Josh hated fighting as much as I did. Some people enjoy arguing and door-banging...'

'Gabby does,' said David, and then surprised them both by admitting slowly, 'And maybe I'm not so different after all. Maybe I'm not as much like Josh as I thought. I did get a bit of a charge out of all that yelling. I didn't want to crawl away and hide, or grovel for her forgiveness just for the sake of peace; I wanted to stand there toe-to-toe and slug it out until we got the problem resolved...'

'OK, then let's get you into the ring, slugger,' said Victoria bracingly, turning to pick up the tattered tights from the floor and collect her bag. David stopped her.

'Just a minute, what's that on your blouse? Is that— is it *blood*?'

'Oh, no! It must have happened when I pricked my fingers on the roses.' Victoria started to brush at the small red spot that stained the cream silk chiffon over her breast, then froze as she realised that her hands were grubby from changing the tyre and there was still a little pearl of blood on her left thumb. She didn't feel like engaging in another discussion on the wisdom of her driving to the party alone so she hastily licked away the blood and dropped her hands by her sides.

'No, that's no good. Here, let me. Sit down.' Thankful he hadn't asked to see the scratches, Victoria let David take out his handkerchief and moisten a corner with his tongue. She even let him undo a few of the tiny buttons concealed by the pintucked front of her blouse so that he could make a pad of part of the handkerchief behind the silk while he dealt with the stain. It was as they sat like this, Victoria leaning back in the chair with her hands tucked out of sight at her sides, David's hair brushing her chin as he bent to his task, that the door opened and Lucas Grey stepped into the room.

'West.'

David reared up as if the single word had been a shot, letting go of the handkerchief which slid down inside Victoria's blouse so that she had to fish blushingly for it under the basilisk black stare.

'Uh—Lucas. We were just——'

'So I see. My sister wants to see you.'

'She does?' David said jerkily and flushed. 'I mean, of course. I want to see her, that's why I'm here. I suppose she told you about our...um...disagreement——'

Lucas Grey said nothing. He looked from the flustered woman in the chair with her tousled hair and her blouse halfway unbuttoned to the discarded tights on the floor and his mouth thinned, accentuating its uneven cut. His gaze, when it returned to David's flushed face, was relentlessly hard.

'She's in my study. She knows you're here, and with whom. I suggest you owe her some kind of explanation. But I warn you, it had better be good. She's not in the mood to be easily placated. Gabrielle may be occasionally hot-headed but she isn't gullible——'

'I—I never thought she was——'

Hearing David reduced to the level of a stammering boy made Victoria cringe inside. The evening had rapidly descended from merely embarrassing to utterly humiliating. Unsteadily Victoria buttoned her blouse, praying she wasn't ruining the delicate fabric with grease-marks. She wondered if she could scoop the tights into her bag without the gimlet-eyed tyrant noticing and decided not. Without even looking at her he managed to give the impression of monitoring her every move.

'Then maybe you're the one who's the fool. If you want a permanent future in Computel you're not going to get there on my sister's back—much less by putting her on her back and holding your hand out.'

Victoria gave a silent gasp and David's hands clenched at the crudely placed blow. 'If you're suggesting——'

'I'm not suggesting anything,' he was told bluntly. 'I'm telling you. This may be a family company, but the members of the family, whether by blood or by marriage, succeed only as far as their merits will take them. And those merits depend on personal integrity as much as business acumen.'

'I've never done anything I've been ashamed of,' said David doggedly.

'Then you're either incredibly amoral or incredibly inexperienced,' said Lucas Grey cynically. 'Neither of which is much recommendation for business or marriage. Now I suggest you find my sister before she decides you're not worth waiting for...'

David immediately forgot his outrage in panic at the thought, and displayed agonised indecision as he looked pleadingly at Victoria. 'Yes, I... Tory, do you think you could——?'

'I'll be all right. Go, David.' Victoria got up and pushed him gently in the direction of the door.

'But I don't like to leave you——'

'Try,' interrupted Lucas Grey silkily, the Canadian drawl crossing the border into Alaska to etch the wintry addition, 'You might be surprised how easy it really is...'

Still David hovered anxiously. 'I...Tory—Victoria isn't involved in this—I don't think you understood earlier, at the door——'

The black eyes flickered briefly. 'Oh, I think I understand perfectly now.'

'Oh, well—I'll introduce you properly when I get back,' David promised, edging nervously towards the door. 'Er...would you look after Victoria? She's a bit shy with strangers——'

'Of course. I'll take *very* good care of Victoria,' Lucas Grey said smoothly, expanding the syllables of her name with soft emphasis as he ushered David out the door. Then, to Victoria's horror, he closed it again and leant on it, an irresistible force against an immovable object. David had only heard the promise in his boss's voice, but Victoria had heard the underlying threat.

There was a small, fraught silence while she wondered what to say. For all its stark definitions, Lucas Grey's face was as unrevealing as a blank canvas.

Victoria touched the top button of her blouse again, checking to make sure the ruffled collar was primly fastened. She cleared her throat.

'I see you've been doing some redecorating.'

A thick black eyebrow lifted and she blushed miserably. What a ridiculous thing to say! Instead of breaking the ice she had skidded ineptly across the surface.

Her blush deepened as he bent down without comment and picked up her tights, studying them with fastidious distaste as they dangled from his hand. Victoria's fingers itched to snatch them off him but her instincts warned her not to make any sudden moves.

'Did you manage to convince him?'

'I beg your pardon?'

'That he can have his cake and eat it, too. Or was a furtive coupling intended to provoke just this kind of confrontation so that he would be forced into breaking things off with Gabrielle? Don't try and tell me that you're madly in love with him because for all your betraying *déshabillé* state a few minutes ago you didn't look very aroused by whatever he was doing to you. A sexy woman like you would *demand* passion from a true love-affair. Therefore I can only assume you're indulging your ego. You must be a very exciting woman and very confident of your power. An ambitious young man like David doesn't take risks like this unless the rewards are very great.'

Sexy? Demanding? A very exciting woman? Who on earth was he talking about? Victoria stared at him, her mouth parted in shock. There had been no sarcasm in his voice but surely he was mocking her, or being deliberately insulting. Either that or he was drunk to the point of hallucinating. There was no sexy, exciting *femme fatale* in the room. Only Victoria.

'You must have had him frantic,' he went on, studying her broodingly as he twirled the ragged tights. 'Does he make a practice of ripping your clothes to shreds? It must be a very costly affair. I would have thought a woman like you would have preferred a little more finesse...'

A woman like her? Victoria closed her mouth as she struggled with his outrageously mistaken image of her. The reason for his ludicrous assumptions was slowly dawning on her. She had been so shocked and disconcerted by his unexpected arrival that she hadn't even considered the scene from his point of view. He had remarked that he knew who she was. But it was glaringly apparent that he didn't, not at all!

She gave in to her instinct and whisked the ruined tights from his hand and pushed them shakily into her handbag. 'Mr Grey——' She stopped. How was she going to explain without sorely embarrassing them both?

'*Mademoiselle?*' He paused mockingly but Victoria was so distracted by his lapse into French that she ignored the implied question. She knew that he was of French-Canadian extraction, so perhaps English wasn't his first language, although he seemed to speak it perfectly...and he was supposed to be a genius, after all. Still, maybe it would be best to put it into words of one syllable...

'This isn't what you think,' she said carefully. 'What you saw when you came in...we weren't—doing what you thought we were doing...' That sounded a little vague, so she added, 'I tore my tights on a rose-bush outside. I was just taking them off——'

'And your blouse? You were taking that off, too?' he enquired, so pleasantly that Victoria wanted to hit him.

'No, of course I wasn't! I had a mark on it. David was trying to get rid of it.'

'Of course! It is obvious that you're totally innocent. It is *my* evil mind that misconstrued the situation...'

'Exactly!' exclaimed Victoria with relief, before she realised that this time he was definitely being sarcastic. She braced herself for another verbal assault.

'You have blood on your mouth.'

'W-what?' Victoria hastily licked her lips and then wished she hadn't because those sinfully dark eyes followed the action with unnerving interest. They weren't black after all, she realised, but very dark brown, shot with paler streaks of hazel. She could see the finer detail because he had moved closer, too close. She backed up a few steps.

He followed.

'It's too soft a mouth to be bitten,' he murmured. 'A lover doesn't have to be rough to be exciting, or is that the way you like it? Does it excite you to coolly make love to another woman's man in her own home, to flaunt his unfaithfulness as a measure of your power? Take care *mademoiselle*: one day you may find yourself fatally ensnared by your own appetites. The pendulum is finally swinging back, and modern society is beginning to frown on extravagant sexual behaviour as being not only morally suspect but potentially lethal——'

Victoria's blush was now brilliant. The man was lecturing her as if she was a brazen hussy who had no self-respect, let alone common sense. At the same time he managed to make her sound wickedly enticing.

Victoria, who had never been forceful, knew she had to stop this nonsense before he addled her brain completely. 'In the first place, Mr Grey, it's *madame*, not *mademoiselle.*' She made the point for the second time that night. 'And my surname happens to be *West*——'

There was an explosive pause. When he spoke it was with quiet ferocity. 'David is married? You're his *wife*?' Somehow his emphasis gave the impression that he found the latter even more outrageous than the former.

'No, of course not! I——'

'His ex-wife?' That idea obviously had only marginally more favour.

'No! I——'

'Sister-in-law?'

Victoria shook her head and subsided, waiting. Maybe he would eventually get there himself.

He didn't have to. Just as he growled, 'Well, who the hell *are* you, Mrs West?' the door was flung open again and David dragged in a tall, dark, handsome young woman whom he thrust at Victoria.

'Here she is,' declared David grimly, releasing the struggling woman, 'wallowing in her appalling sin. Gabby, I'd like you to meet Victoria.

'Mother, this is the jealous witch who refuses to marry me because she thinks you're my mistress!'

CHAPTER TWO

'*MOTHER?*'

The chorus was equal parts shock and disbelief. Gabrielle Grey's brown eyes glowed with scorn as she let out an angry laugh. Her brother, on the other hand, looked from David to Victoria with an arrested expression of intense curiosity.

'If she's your loving mother, I'm your maiden aunt!' Gabrielle snapped, tossing her long midnight locks to express her defiance in the fact of such a blatant lie.

'You must have still been in nappies when you got pregnant,' murmured Lucas drily, and Victoria blushed. The tender way that he said 'pregnant' in that warm, smoky voice made her stomach flutter.

'Stepmother, actually,' David was telling Gabrielle roundly. 'And yes, she is—very loving. I was eighteen when my mother died but it didn't make losing her any easier, and it was even tougher on my father and younger brothers and sisters. If it hadn't been for the support and understanding that Victoria gave the younger ones when they were acting out their anger the family probably would have drifted apart at the seams. Even before she married Dad we thought of her as one of us, and afterwards she never once made us feel in the way, or a burden, no matter how tired or upset she was herself. If nothing else I owe her my respect and loyalty for what she did, and is still doing, for the family, and I expect those I love to show her just as much respect!'

By the time this flattering paean was through Victoria was aflame with embarrassment. If there was any way guaranteed to set your beloved against her mother-in-law it was to imply that she was a candidate for sainthood. Victoria wouldn't blame Gabrielle if she dug her heels in now, out of sheer pride. She would probably never forgive Victoria for putting her through the humiliation of this moment. 'Mother-in-law...' Victoria mentally choked on the image that the word traditionally provoked...that of a demanding battle-axe who could never be satisfied. She really wasn't ready for this...any of it. She looked sideways at the man beside her. He was still looking at her in that uncomfortably speculative way and there was a suspicious tug at the corner of his mouth, as if he found the situation vastly amusing. For the life of her, Victoria couldn't think of a single thing to say to ease the ghastly awkwardness of the moment.

'Gabrielle had decided to surprise me by meeting me at the airport this afternoon,' David told Victoria with clipped restraint. 'Only *she* got the surprise because, lo and behold, she saw me already being very warmly welcomed by another young woman, one whom I promptly gave that pendant to. I was tried, found guilty and executed on the spot!'

'He said that he was buying the pendant for his mother,' said Gabrielle stiffly, not looking at Victoria.

'Oh, I see,' murmured Victoria, pleating her skirt with her hand, as she remembered the way she had hugged David when they met outside the Customs hall, the way he had whirled her around in his arms and given her a smacking kiss. 'It was a mistake anyone could make...'

'Especially since David hadn't told me anything about you,' said Gabrielle sullenly, looking at her at last, defiance still burning in the slanted brown eyes. 'All I knew about his family was that his father had been a history professor, that his brother Jason still lived at home with his mother and that his two sisters are on a working holiday in Australia.'

'And the other brother?'

David frowned, disconcerted by Lucas's irrelevant interruption. 'Who?'

'You mentioned younger brothers, in the plural; Jason, whom I believe you once said is at law school—and who is the other...?'

Victoria stiffened, the pleats falling out of her trembling hand. David shot her a quick look of guilt and concern.

'We lost Steven and Dad about the same time, four years ago,' he said with stony reluctance.

Victoria's flush paled and she opened her mouth, and closed it again as she saw the familiar expression of blank rejection etching David's features. He, of all Joshua's children, was the one who missed his presence in their daily lives most keenly. Victoria had been helpless to ease his anger—and guilt...

'An accident?' Lucas Grey, it seemed, had no qualms about probing what was an obvious wound.

'Kidney failure in Steven's case,' said David stiffly. 'He was born with spina bifida and was quite severely physically handicapped. Dad was...he was in a car accident a few months after Steven died.'

'It must have been a difficult time for you.' The sympathy, however, was tempered by that inexorable curiosity. 'How old was your brother?'

David, it seemed, had no more idea than Victoria where all this was leading. He shrugged. 'Five.'

Gabrielle gave a soft gasp and made a tentative movement towards him, but withdrew as he gave her a glare that showed he had not forgiven her for her distrust.

'A big gap,' Lucas commented, and then took Victoria's breath away by turning his dark eyes on her, pinning her with his intense interest as he asked flatly, 'Was he your son?'

Every bone in her body ached with the echo of loss. 'Yes,' she said with proud dignity. 'He was my son. But if you're asking me if I was his birth mother then the answer is no. He was Miranda's son—Joshua's first wife...all the children are Miranda's.'

'Victoria.' David deliberately moved himself between Lucas and his stepmother, shooting his boss a warning look. 'You don't have to——'

'It's all right, David,' she reassured him quietly. 'I suppose under the circumstances it's only natural that

Mr Grey should be interested in your family background...'

'So you took on a ready-made family—of five?—when you married David's father. You must have loved him very much.'

Victoria looked down, discovering she was pleating her skirt again. Hastily she smoothed out the crumples. 'Yes, I did,' she murmured tautly.

'If you want to ask any more questions, Lucas, you can ask me,' said David roughly. 'Leave Victoria alone.'

Lucas raised his eyebrows at the bristling protectiveness. 'Surely you didn't expect to introduce us to your unusually young stepmother and *not* have us ask questions? In fact, until this misunderstanding occurred I suppose you might have rather looked forward to the polite consternation this meeting would cause...'

David had the grace to look discomfited and Gabrielle pounced on the chance to retrieve her dignity.

'The way you've always talked about your mother, I thought that she was a comfortable middle-aged housewife, not...well, she doesn't look a day older than you!'

'She isn't. In fact she's a year younger than I am.' David rallied valiantly. 'But that's not quite the point. The point is that you didn't even trust me enough to confront me with what you saw. You just skirted around it with vague accusations that I didn't have a hope of refuting——'

'Well, what did you expect? That I would lay myself bare for you to trample all over? I've been that route before. And how would *you* react if you'd seen *me* kissing and hugging and giving expensive presents to a man you'd never even seen before?'

'I would have discovered the facts before I waded in with the accusations.'

The battle showed every sign of heating up again and Victoria instinctively assumed her normal role of peacemaker. 'Oh, David, you know that's not completely true. You're talking about logic, not feelings. If you were being purely logical about things you would have discussed the problem sensibly with Gabrielle, instead of shooting counter-accusations with her.'

'Are you telling me you're on *her* side?' demanded David incredulously.

'I'm not on anyone's side, David. It seems to me as if I'm the meat inside the sandwich. You hadn't been entirely frank with Gabrielle so you can't object if she responds with an equal lack of openness, can you?' She turned to Gabrielle and said quietly, 'Perhaps one day we can laugh about the way we met. But I think it might be better if I skipped dinner tonight——'

'No!'

The reaction was unanimous, but from the varying expressions it was obvious that the reasons were very different. Victoria sensed that David wanted to rub his erstwhile fiancée's nose in her mistake, while Gabrielle wanted a buffer against his aggressive self-righteousness. Lucas Grey was the only one whose motive was a mystery, and Victoria wasn't game even to make a guess.

'I'm really very sorry if we've embarrassed you,' Gabrielle said in a little formal rush, apparently finding it easier to apologise to Victoria than to David. She held out her hand and, after a brief hesitation, Victoria quickly shook it.

Not quickly enough. As their hands dropped away from each other Gabrielle looked down and gave a small exclamation of surprise at the grey smudge left on her soft palm.

'Oh, dear, I'm very sorry.' It was Victoria's turn to be mortified. 'I... I should have washed as soon as I arrived...'

'Why? Victoria—your hands!' David was aghast all over again as he finally noticed their true state. 'Where did all that grime come from?'

He made her sound like a ragged street urchin. Victoria clasped her hands together, careful to keep them away from her clothes as everyone stared at them. 'I...is there somewhere I could wash them?' She smiled a politely blind smile at the curious Gabrielle.

She should have known that David wouldn't be satisfied with the evasion. He took her wrists possessively and turned them over so that they could all see the extent of the damage. 'Tory—they look positively battered! Surely you didn't do all this on a rose-bush?'

'Well, no...' said Victoria awkwardly, wishing he wouldn't make such a fuss.

'If I didn't know you better I'd say you'd been in a brawl,' David went on. 'What on earth have you been up to, Tory? Is this why you were late?'

She sighed. David was as stubborn as a bulldog when he got his teeth into a puzzle. 'Yes... I had a flat tyre, that's all. Is there a bathroom on the ground floor?'

David didn't give Gabrielle a time to reply. 'A flat tyre! Where? When?'

'A few streets away——'

'Did you call the AA?'

'No, I didn't. It was only a flat tyre, David.'

'You changed it yourself! In the dark!' He couldn't have sounded more horrified if she'd said she had robbed a bank.

'It wasn't quite dark. I——'

'Have you ever changed one before?'

'No. But you don't need a degree in mechanical engineering to change a tyre. There was a very clear instruction book in the car.'

'But the jack, how did you manage that——?'

'It operates on a very simple principle, David. Even a moron could understand it.' Victoria was beginning to let her exasperation with his attitude show in her soft voice. He was making her sound like the ultimate helpless female, incapable of solving the simplest of problems without male help. It was irritating enough to cope with his over-protectiveness in private, let alone in company.

'But how did you get the wheel-nuts off?' David sounded just as exasperated, as if her ability to cope was a slight on his masculinity.

'I'm stronger than I look,' said Victoria stoutly. To her annoyance she saw a smile flicker across Lucas Grey's sexy mouth. Was he as aggravatingly chauvinistic as

David could be sometimes? She had deliberately not looked at him before but now she lifted her soft chin and gave him what she hoped was a quelling stare that told him he could keep his opinions—both verbal and non-verbal—to himself. He must have got the message because he stood silently and unhelpfully by as David insisted on dragging a step-by-step account out of her.

When she finished David said grudgingly. 'Well, it sounds as if you did OK, but I think I should drive you home. I'll come back tomorrow and check the wheel before you drive the car again.'

Victoria compressed her mouth, knowing it was useless to argue. He would find that the wheel was fine—despite her inexperience, she trusted her own workmanship—but he wouldn't feel he had fulfilled his responsibilities as her self-appointed protector until he had done it.

'Come on,' he continued. 'We'll find the bathroom and put something on those scratches. They might get infected if you leave them....'

Victoria briefly closed her eyes at the contemplation of losing another tussle of wills. A mistake.

'You aren't feeling faint or anything, are you, Tory?' David asked anxiously, taking her elbow in his grasp.

'I think I feel a fit of the vapours coming on,' she said drily. She was sorry as soon as the words passed her lips because both David and Gabrielle seemed to take her seriously. Only Lucas Grey seemed amused.

'How Victorian of you, Victoria.' He took her other elbow. 'Why don't I see to your stepmother's wounds, David? I think you and Gabby should sort out your own problems before you start attacking other people's. And after you've settled them I suggest you go and entertain our other guests. They must be getting hungry by now, if not curious, and we can satisfy one if not the other. Tell Iris to serve the soup, Gabby, while Victoria and I look out the smelling salts.'

David didn't immediately let her go and for a few seconds Victoria had the unwelcome experience of feeling like a bone between two bristling dogs.

'Or perhaps you don't trust me to treat your stepmother with the same kind of thoughtful consideration you show my sister?' murmured Lucas smoothly, catching David on the raw with the combined challenge and reproach.

'You really don't have to do this,' Victoria insisted feverishly, as she was escorted along the polished floor of the hallway.

'What kind of host would I be if I didn't? After you.'

Victoria balked at the wide doors of a lift. 'Isn't there a bathroom on the ground floor?'

'Yes, but the medical supplies are upstairs.' He applied a very slight, interesting pressure to the bones of her elbow that made her hurriedly step out of his grasp and into the lift. He followed her and pushed the single button.

'Isn't it a bit extravagant to have a lift like this in a two-storeyed house?' she said faintly, unnerved by the hush in the large square box. The floor of the lift was the same polished wood as the hall had been, but the walls and ceiling were fully lined with plush grey-blue carpet that seemed to absorb every sound. The necessary control panel and fittings were in brass—or perhaps it was gold-plate!—and polished to a high finish. On the side walls were matching full-length gold-framed mirrors which gave the unnerving impression that she was sharing the lift with an infinite number of dark and dangerously attractive Lucas Greys. As if one was not enough for her senses to cope with! The infinity of Victorias dwindled into insignificance, swamped by all that dominating masculinity.

'In the circumstances it was a necessity, and where necessities are concerned I'm an extravagant man. If you must have, you may as well have the best.'

'If you can afford it,' said Victoria stiffly, not sure whether to approve or be appalled by the philosophy.

'The best isn't always the most expensive, Victoria,' he reproved her gently, propping a flat hand against the front wall and leaning on it so that he could look openly at her delicate profile. 'Sometimes the best can cost you nothing. For example, the best thing that you could give me right now is a smile.'

Surprised into looking at him, she blushed at the warm invitation to amusement in his brown eyes.

'A smile of gratitude if nothing else. I did, after all, rescue you from the clutches of your over-anxious stepson. Does he always treat you like that?'

'Like what?' Victoria instantly bristled.

'Like a very fragile angel who has to be constantly guarded against the slings and arrows of fortune, outrageous and otherwise.'

She wanted to be offended, but how could she when he had seen the truth of it for himself?

'Since his father...David takes his responsibilities very seriously...' she mumbled, looking away.

'So I noticed. And you're his responsibility?'

'I'm my own responsibility,' she said stiffly.

'Then why do you let him get away with it?'

That was something she couldn't possibly explain, not when David had given her such a clear indication that he didn't want her to.

'This lift seems to be terribly slow,' she said.

He dropped his hand from the wall and she realised that he had been deliberately leaning on the control panel that controlled the opening of the door. It slid back soundlessly and she quickly stepped out, a strange prickly sensation running up and down her spine as he moved out behind her. She turned too quickly, almost stumbling on her heels and he raised his eyebrows at her.

'I wasn't going to touch you,' he said.

'I didn't think you were,' she lied.

'Of course you didn't,' he said soothingly, in a tone that reeked of disbelief.

'If you'll show me where the bathroom is, I'll be as fast as I can,' she said desperately.

He strolled past her, giving her an exaggeratedly wide berth that annoyed her even more than the lingering amusement curling his mouth.

When she realised that the room he had guided her into wasn't a bathroom she stopped dead, looking at the expanse of deep-pile blue carpet and the dramatic wall-paper of a deeper blue peppered with small maroon geometric shapes. A single chair was the only free-standing furniture. Along one wall was a full-length walk-in wardrobe, the maroon folding doors partly open to reveal racks of suits and shelves stacked with sweaters and masculine shoes. The bed was unlike any that Victoria had ever seen before, even in the interior decoration books and magazines she enjoyed getting from the library. It was sunk completely into the floor, carpeted shelving scattered with books, tapes and papers recessed around its perimeter, the huge, billowy soft bed taking up the entire sunken space. The duvet and numerous pillows and cushions were navy blue, with strips of the same geometric pattern as the wallpaper, and a matching fabric had been used for the curtains that framed the full-length french windows that opened out on to a small balcony at the back of the house. From the middle of the room Victoria could just see the dark glitter of the Tamaki Estuary beyond the grounds.

Altogether it was a relentlessly masculine room, uncompromisingly luxurious and yet almost spartan in its tastefulness.

'Whose room is this?' she asked, although she already knew.

'We have four first-floor bedrooms. This is a spare.'

Even if it had have been possible for so cynical and sexy a man to look innocent, his blandly wide-eyed expression would not have fooled her. The gaping bed-pit yawned even wider than ever at her feet. She stepped back.

'It's your room, isn't it?' she demanded severely.

He smiled, not at all abashed by his ridiculous lie, mocking her nervousness. 'Yes. Do you like it?'

She loved it! 'It's very...interesting,' she said primly. 'But you were going to take me to the bathroom.'

'I know. It's through here.' He slid back a door which she hadn't noticed because it was wallpapered to match the room, the small handle a three-dimensional version of the geometric pattern.

Victoria cleared her dry throat. 'Isn't there another one?'

'Does it make you nervous to be in my bedroom? Surely you don't think I'd take advantage of your misfortune?'

He was so obviously enjoying her discomfiture that Victoria was visited by a rare moment of impulsive mischief. 'You mean it's considered a misfortune to be in your bedroom?' she asked mildly.

He laughed, the hard angles of his face breaking up into attractive curves. 'For an angel, perhaps it is. Unless you're here to reform me. They do say that reformed rakes make the best husbands, don't they?'

'No. They say that they make the *strictest* husbands,' said Victoria, regretting she had been side-tracked into the unexpected byplay about rakes and husbands but unable to resist adding stuffily, 'Personally, I don't see that it's a woman's place to reform a man. If he's capable of reforming he should do it himself.'

'You're right, of course,' he agreed meekly. 'But sometimes a man needs the right incentive.'

'This is all very amusing, but I don't think it's getting us anywhere,' she replied sharply.

'Oh, I don't know,' he murmured, studying her distress with fascinated amusement. No doubt she thought she looked stern and assertive with that haughty expression, but her soft mouth and uncertain eyes with their strange rust-green flecks totally ruined the effect. Not to mention the freckles and the wild blush that arose every time he stared at her for any length of time. He knew any number of women who couldn't blush at the most arrant obscenity, let alone a relatively chaste look. No wonder her stepson was driven to hover over her like an anxious hen over a wayward chick. There was a gentle air of serene, dreamy innocence about her that made it difficult to think of her as an ordinary wife and mother dealing with the everyday hassles of life. But of course she *wasn't* ordinary. She had married a man who must have been considerably older than herself and taken on the care of five children not her own, apparently acquitting herself with honour on both counts, judging from David's attitude. A fleeting thought briefly invaded the rosy picture. Was it possible that one or other, or both of them, had fallen in love but were denying it out of loyalty to the memory of David's father? Lucas watched Victoria's eyes stubbornly refuse to slide away from his, even though every line of her body suggested she'd like nothing better than to disappear into thin air, and decided, no, that air of innocence wasn't feigned. There were a few odd undercurrents to their relationship but they definitely weren't sexual. She had dealt with David's over-reaction with an understanding kindness and genuine affection that hadn't quite concealed her faint underlying irritation at his intrusion on her independence. Passion, tension and excitement had been conspicuous by their absence. Unlike now.

Lucas smiled faintly to himself. He was, by virtue of his intelligence and profession, a very rational man—which made his occasional outbursts of passionate irrationalism all the more exhilarating when they occurred. At the moment he was possessed by the very irrational desire to lift the angel's halo and peek underneath it, to find out what it was about this gentle, innocuous, ginger-skinned woman that made him ache with a combination of lust and uncertainty, like a schoolboy in the grip of his first crush. He had thought it was a once-in-a-lifetime feeling and yet here he was, a mature, experienced man, struck by the same helpless, boyish thrill, the sudden desire to do something swaggeringly impressive in front of the unwitting object of his desire. The difference was that when he was fourteen and passionately in love with his ripely gorgeous maths teacher actual consummation had been out of the question, and hot-blooded fantasy far more exciting than awkward reality would no doubt have been.

'You wash your hands, I'll find the disinfectant for those scratches,' he told her abruptly, suddenly uncomfortable with his thoughts, but Victoria wasn't even aware of him, let alone affected by his mental ravishment. She was looking at their new surroundings in

awe. At least his *house* impressed her, thought Lucas
wryly, put firmly in his place.

In contrast to the sunken bed in the room behind them,
the bath was raised. The black and white tiled floor as-
cended three steps across its full width to the long, deep
black marble bath with its elegant black and silver fittings. The walls were also tiled in gleaming black and
from random lighting niches ferns and exotically
flowering hot-house plants spilled in profusion, some
almost reaching the floor. The black ceiling gave an oddly
disorientating impression of endless space aided by the
metre-high mirror strip that wrapped around the room
at chest height and, like the lift, reflected multiple images
of the room's occupants. At the other end of the
bathroom was a stark, open shower with a snake-like
silver removable shower-head, no curtain or screen to
preserve the user's modesty—assuming there was any
point in trying to be modest in this voyeuristic dream of
a bathroom! In between the bath and the shower were
a black pedestal basin, toilet and bidet and more illumi-
nated recesses stored white bath-linen and toiletries. The
subdued lights in the niches had come on automatically
when Lucas opened the door and now he flicked a switch
which turned on black strip-lights on the wall above the
bath and basin.

'The basin tap has a thermostat mixer and sensor; you
don't even have to touch it. Just hold your hands underneath it.'

When Victoria still didn't move, Lucas made a quiet
sound of irritation and guided her over to the basin with
a firm hand on her back. Before she could react he took
her bag out of her absent grasp, hung it beside a white
towelling bathrobe on the wall and guided her hands
under the single tap. Warm water foamed out of the
graceful silver arch and Lucas poured some liquid soap
into his hand and transferred it to her palms as he began
to softly massage them under the cleansing stream.

'I can do that,' said Victoria hastily recovering, jerking
her hands away, alarmed by his gentleness. 'Oh!'

Her gesture had splashed soapy water over both of them. Was she *ever* going to stop making an idiot of herself in front of this man? She gave him an agonised look. 'I'm very sorry, I...I hope it doesn't leave a mark.' She didn't know what fabric his dinner-jacket was made of but it looked suspiciously like silk. 'If it does you must send me the cleaning bill...'

'It's only a few drops. I'm sure it'll dry out in no time,' he said soothingly. 'Just finish washing and then we'll take a look at those scratches. There's a soft scrubbing brush in the wall above the basin, if you need it.'

'Thank you.'

Victoria did need it. When she had dealt with the marks on her hands she looked in dismay at her short, unpainted nails. Grease was deeply ingrained behind several of them and no amount of scrubbing appeared able to shift it. No stockings and a mark on her blouse she could just about cope with, but dirty fingernails would put her beyond the pale at the dinner table. She quickly turned her hands over as Lucas stopped sorting through the bottles and tubes recessed above the mirror and turned back to her.

'Hmm. A couple of those look quite deep,' he said, inspecting the scratches. 'This might sting a little, but it'll do the trick.'

'I can do it,' said Victoria as he uncapped the small bottle, not daring to pull on her hands this time.

'So can I,' he told her firmly, tipping the contents on to a cotton wool ball and cupping her hand to hold it steady as he dabbed. Victoria was proud of the daintiness of her hands and feet, it was her one vanity, but it wasn't vanity that made her suddenly short of breath. His hands were so much bigger than hers that she half expected him to be clumsy, but his fingers moved with extraordinary precision as he traced the scratches and she suddenly had a vision of him cradling a baby with that same tender delicacy. She looked at his mouth, which was tucked into a concentrated line, faintly stern. Hard. How ridiculous to think of him with a baby... as a father. He was an unrepentant bachelor, from what

David had said, married to his work and only dating women who were prepared to accept their subordinate place in his life gracefully. Babies didn't come into the equation anywhere. Lucas Grey and babies... making babies with Lucas Grey... Victoria went hot at the very idea.

'Am I hurting you?' Lucas asked, registering her sudden tension but thankfully not looking up from his task.

'No.' She looked at herself in the mirror to try and take her mind off that warm hand lightly but securely restraining hers. Her hair looked like a haystack, she noticed wryly. The reflections in the room caused the light to bounce off the unruly strands at odd angles, and for the first time she noticed the hint of autumn in the plain brown locks, the redhead she might have been if she had inherited her mother's true colouring—not just her infinity of freckles. Monica Bailey had long, dark red hair that even as a child Victoria had envied. She still vividly recalled visiting her mother in hospital after her first cerebral haemorrhage and being told by her father that beneath the bandages her head had been shaved. To her child's mind that discovery had been a devastating portent of the news, a few days later, that her mother had died. To this day Victoria disliked having her hair cut. If it wasn't for the fact that once it grew below her shoulders her thick, wavy hair acquired the consistency of wool, Victoria wouldn't set foot in a hairdressing salon. She was due for a cut now, but she had been putting it off.

'Are you sure? You look a little pale?' He had joined her in the study of her reflection. Thank goodness she had stopped blushing.

'My hair is a mess,' she blurted out, and to her chagrin he side kindly,

'Would you like me to lend you a brush?'

'I have a comb in my bag,' she said quickly, horrified at the thought of sharing something as intimate as a hairbrush with him.

She dragged the comb through the tangles as Lucas disposed of the soiled cotton wool and bottle of disinfectant, and was slightly reassured by the result. Her nails, though, mocked her with their unsightliness. She sighed.

'What's the matter?'

'Nothing.' He had the look of a man who was never satisfied with polite platitudes and Victoria sighed again, inwardly this time. 'My nails. Do you think people will notice?'

He looked at them. 'Yes.'

'Oh.' He obviously didn't deliver polite platitudes either.

'Just a minute. I think I have the solution.'

He disappeared, and when he came back a few minutes later he was carrying a small cream case which he unzipped, revealing a stunningly well-equipped manicure set, including at least a dozen bottles of nail polish and a battery-operated nail-dryer.

'Gabrielle's,' said Lucas. 'In the circumstances I don't think she'd mind you using it.' He selected one of the small bottles and showed her the label. 'Flirty Red'. 'This colour, I think.'

Victoria was taken aback. 'Oh, I don't think—that is, I never wear nail polish...' It hardly seemed worth the bother when her nails were so short, even though she took care to make sure they were well-shaped.

'Perhaps, just this once, you might make an exception to that rule. Nobody's going to think you're a scarlet woman just because you wear polish, Victoria.'

He made her sound like a dried-up old prude. 'It isn't a rule, I just...' She trailed off, annoyed that he had put her on the defensive with his gentle mockery. 'I'd rather have that colour.' She pointed to a more subdued shade.

'Don't you trust my taste?'

'No.'

He picked up the bottle of her choice and read the label. He grinned that fascinatingly sexy grin. 'OK, "Passionate Plum" it is.'

Victoria sat on the bath steps and tried to ignore him as she began to apply the polish, but it was impossible when he sat down beside her to watch. She could hear his slow, steady breathing, and when he tilted his head closer her hand jerked nervously.

'You've gone over the edge a bit there,' he said helpfully.

'I can see that.' She stopped what she was doing. 'Don't you have something else to do?'

'No.'

'Well, find something. I can't concentrate with you breathing all over me?'

'*All* over you?' he murmured, the dark brown eyes wandering expressively. But he got up and wandered away. Victoria bit her tongue as she tried to steady her inexpert brush, frowning in concentration as she finished her left hand. It didn't look *too* bad, she thought, until her host came over and made an odd strangled sound.

'Look, why don't you let me do it?' he said, firmly detaching the brush from her trembling hand. 'I certainly can't do any worse.'

Victoria was so taken aback she let him briskly remove the evidence of her inexpertise with polish remover before she found her tongue. 'I suppose you're an expert at painting women's fingernails?' she said sarcastically as he uncapped the bottle again, splaying her fingers with his.

'Actually toenails are more in my line,' he replied mildly. 'But I'm sure the technique is the same.'

'You've worked in a beauty parlour?' Victoria said foolishly, watching him rapidly accomplish what had taken her long minutes of painstaking care. Too late she realised the extent of the intimacy she had permitted him, and not only physically.

'My services have been on a more...personal basis,' he said, his brief hesitation making Victoria go hot inside. She had no difficulty at all picturing the personal services involved. She could just see him lounging in that sunken bed next door, pampering some nude odalisque with sinful little personal luxuries, smoothing lotion over her glowing skin, brushing her thick brown hair with slow, sensual strokes and painting her toenails, prettying her up for their mutual pleasure. He would probably be nude, too, and she would——

'Victoria?'

'What?' She blinked, realising that he had been talking and she hadn't heard a word. It was getting to be a habit in his company, drifting off into an abstraction until he was forced to nudge her out of it.

'You can put that hand under the drier now, while I do the other,' he repeated patiently.

'Oh. Th-thank you.' She did as she was told. The faster her nails were done, the sooner they would safely be back in company.

'You must have been very young when you married David's father.'

She resented him furiously for the trapped feeling his sudden question engendered. 'Eighteen.'

'And your parents approved?' It was obvious he didn't. Well, it was none of his business, but she told him anyway.

'I didn't have any parents. My mother died when I was twelve and my father when I was sixteen.'

'Who looked after you? Where did you live after he died?'

The other hand was dry now, so Victoria felt free to pay him back. 'I moved in with Joshua and Miranda.'

She rose, noting with some satisfaction that she had managed to shock him. 'You mean you lived with David's father when he was still married to his first wife?'

Victoria nodded steadily. 'I sort of kept house for them. And when Miranda died I married Josh.'

And let him make what he wished of that bald encapsulation of the facts! Victoria unhooked her bag and tucked it under her arm as she moved to the door.

Belatedly Lucas was hot on her heels. 'The three of you lived together?' he growled incredulously.

'The eight of us,' Victoria corrected him. 'All the children lived at home then.'

'My God...' The appalled murmur was followed up by a further growl. 'He must have been forty if he was a day... and you were under his care. What in the hell did the authorities have to say about it?'

'He was forty-five when we got married and it was nothing to do with the authorities. I was over age, I could marry whomever I liked.' Victoria had spied the stairs and decided she had no intention of being locked in that luxury-lined box with Lucas Grey, particularly not when he was in this aggressive mood. She had been foolish to think she could provoke him and get away with it, and it was entirely her fault that he thought the worst of poor Josh.

'Only just over age. What happened, Victoria? Did he seduce you when you were vulnerable and then use guilt to get you to step into his wife's shoes——?'

Halfway down the stairs Victoria halted to repair the damage she had done with her little flourish of defiance. 'No, he didn't. For your information, Joshua was always a perfect gentleman. If you had known him you would realise how ridiculous the idea is that he would seduce anyone...'

'What in the hell does that mean?' He halted one step below her, his piercing eyes level with hers. 'Was he impotent when he married you?'

Victoria blushed angrily. 'You have no right to ask me questions like that. I don't even know you!'

He shrugged impatiently. 'Was he?'

'No!'

'But you didn't have any children of your own——'

She looked hard at the wall behind his head, her defiance swamped by an ache of regret. 'We weren't trying, at least, not until just before... before Josh had his accident,' she said huskily.

His anger vanished like smoke and he gently touched her cheek to draw her attention back to himself. 'Oh, Victoria, I'm sorry. I didn't mean to force you to relive sad memories...'

It was her turn to look incredulous and he scowled. 'I was just curious, that's all. *You* made me curious.'

'Oh, I see. So now it's *my* fault you're so offensive.'

'Not offensive. Interested.'

Victoria opened her mouth to tell him what he could do with his interest, in very ladylike terms, of course, when there was a swooshing sound from below.

They both looked down at the man in the wheelchair who had rolled up to the bottom step, his lined, weathered face creased in welcome as he grinned up at them.

'Well, well, well, how lovely to see you again so un-expectedly! Come down and let me introduce you around!'

Lucas said something uncomplimentary in French under his breath then raised his voice. 'There's no need to be sarcastic, Dad; I haven't been away from the party *that* long. As a matter of fact there's someone here I'd like *you* to meet. You'll never guess who.'

Oh, yes, he will! thought Victoria in numb horror, wondering if this whole night would turn out merely to be one long, particularly unpleasant dream. She hoped so. She very badly wanted the familiar man in the wheelchair to be a figment of her own guilt-ridden imagination!

CHAPTER THREE

TWELVE hours later the memory of that ghastly moment still had the power to make Victoria's stomach clench. For a few seconds she had panicked, and in those few seconds the die had been cast.

'Victoria, may I present my stepfather, Scott Sinclair? Scott, this is Victoria West, David's stepmother.'

'*David's* stepmother! You mean——?'

The man in the wheelchair had suddenly burst out laughing and Victoria had quickly stuck her hand out, cutting him off.

'I'm very pleased to meet you, Mr Sinclair,' she had said firmly and precisely, her eyes silently begging him to go along with the charade.

'Huh?' He'd looked from her to his stepson. 'Oh, of course, of course—delighted, I'm sure.' He had shaken hands with her in a parody of politeness, still grinning, his fingers pressing against hers in a secret signal that made her instantly aware of the stupidity of her impulsive action.

'What's the big joke, Dad?' Lucas Grey's voice had had an edge that banished thoughts of confession. She hadn't wanted to provoke a family squabble in the middle of a dinner party.

'Oh . . . just all of us being step-something. It tickled my fancy, that's all, meeting out here by the *stairs* . . .' He'd chuckled again, ostensibly at his weak pun. 'How about wheeling me into dinner, Victoria, so we can get acquainted? Although I have the strangest feeling that I know you already . . .' His eyes had twinkled knowingly at her blush, and she had known she only had herself to blame for the ordeal to come . . .

Victoria closed her eyes now to shut out the sight of fried eggs and bacon sliding out of the pan on to a plate.

'Is that for me? Thanks.' The plate was whisked out of her hand as Jason blundered into the kitchen in his usual early morning fog. He sat down at the breakfast-bar and opened a text book beside him as he began to eat. 'David gone already?'

Victoria nodded. He had left early, full of the fact that his love-life was back on its uneven keel, in order to check on her small car, which now sat in the Greys' huge triple garage, looking very out of place in between a blood-red Jaguar Coupé and a classy white BMW. David had not only insisted on driving the car there himself after the party, but had then kindly taken time out to tell her that in his opinion the clutch and brake needed adjusting and it was time she had it serviced.

'Enjoy yourself last night?' Jason asked absently, already lost in the intricacies of the law.

'No, I had a lousy time.'

'Good...good.' As Victoria expected, Jason's nose remained deeply buried in his book, one hand straying to feel for the coffee which she obligingly slid into his reach.

Victoria finished wrapping the sandwiches she had cut for him and put them in the bulging, battered bag he had dropped on the blue and white tiled floor of the kitchen. She smiled wryly at the bent head. Like his brother, Jason had inherited his father's strong phys-ique and his mother's fairness but, unlike David, he had also inherited his father's academic brilliance. He was serious, dedicated and meticulous to a fault in his studies, and Victoria sometimes wished that his single-minded pursuit of excellence would extend a bit further into his private life. Away from his precious books Jason was incredibly disorganised.

He suddenly looked up at the clock. 'Hell, look at the time—I've got a lecture at nine!' He swiped the last piece of toast around his plate and crammed it into his mouth. 'I don't suppose you've made me any lunch——?'

'In your bag.' They went through the same panicked ritual every morning.

From the kitchen she watched him make a mad dash up the long drive towards the bus stop across the road, crushing down her restless feeling of envy. He had such an air of youthful, eager purpose.

Well, she was youthful too, she told herself, turning back to the dishes. At twenty-five she was only three years older than Jason and one day soon she too would be rushing purposefully off in the mornings instead of letting the days drift by keeping an empty house clean and tidy. She didn't dislike housework; on the contrary, she liked organising and running a busy household, and when the girls had lived at home there had always seemed plenty to do. Since they had left, however, she had realised how achingly empty her own life was, how boring and complacent she was in danger of becoming, behaving like a middle-aged matron instead of a young woman in her prime!

To that end she had secretly begun combing the vacancy ads, knowing that David and Jason, and probably the girls too, would be horrified at the thought of her going out to work. Even though they had left home Tracey and Maxine insisted on sending their contribution to the family budget. It was a matter of honour among them that they gave Victoria all the support they could and made sure that she wanted for nothing. But Victoria found that she *did* want. She was tired of being cocooned from real life by their love and gratitude and, yes, even their guilt.

The trouble was, she had discovered as she had studied the employment ads, she had no academic qualifications, no outside work-experience, no training and no burning desire to learn a new career! She had never been much of a scholar and leaving school at fifteen to look after her ailing father had been a relief rather than a sacrifice.

But there was one marketable skill she *did* possess, one type of job she *could* apply for with complete confidence. It wasn't glamorous or exciting, but it was honest employment and she would actually be getting paid for something she liked doing! There were plenty of advertisements for part-time housekeepers or child-minders in the paper. Given the fact that the rest of the family were all professionals—Maxine an accountant and Tracey a journalist—they would probably be horrified by her choice of job, but Victoria intended to stick to her guns and firmly point out that it was her *own* pride that was important here, not theirs.

She had applied for several advertised jobs but it was a weak moment of uncharacteristic frivolity that had brought her unexpected success. It had been in the Personal rather than the Help Wanted column: 'WANTED—PART-TIME WIFE,' it had said, and she had read on out of pure curiosity.

> Companion-housekeeper wanted to do battle with cantankerous old cripple, view: definitely not marriage! Qualifications: sense of humour, guts, loyalty, patience of a saint—soul of a sinner. Must be willing to pander to employer's every whim, deal with interfering relatives, play good hand of poker. No wowsers, no pity, no quarter. Hours negotiable. Apply with photograph...

Victoria had been smiling when she had reached the final box number, but the desperation implicit between the wicked, biting lines had prompted her, for the first time in her life, to act with rash disregard for the consequences. Her wryly humorous response had received a rapid reply and after several phone calls she had finally met Scott, at his suggestion over lunch in a local park, and learned that he had placed the tongue-in-cheek ad without the knowledge of the son and daughter with whom he lived. The fact that she had responded with similar secrecy had amused them both and confirmed their initial empathy. Victoria found him stubborn and unpredictable, but not as cantankerous as he had claimed nor as elderly as she had expected. Apart from his handicap he appeared to be a fairly fit sixty-five-year-old. Although confined to a wheelchair following a construction accident ten years before, Scott was not a paraplegic and possessed just sufficient movement in his crushed legs to take care of his most personal needs. He wanted a housekeeper for the separate apartments that he maintained within the family home, a lively companion rather than the string of 'bossy' nurses his family had been foisting upon him.

To Victoria it had seemed like the perfect job. Too perfect to be true, as last night had proven. In retrospect the whole evening had been a disaster, starting badly and rapidly going downhill ... !

As the three of them had joined the others at dinner Victoria had known Scott deserved an explanation, although he had probably already guessed the reason for her ridiculous behaviour. Fortunately there had turned out to be a spare setting next to the empty slot for his wheelchair, and Victoria had quickly availed herself of it. Only when she was seated had she realised that she was at the head of the table. She had shrunk down into her chair, pretending to be oblivious to the way that her host hovered behind her for several startled seconds before politely withdrawing to the only other remaining seat, halfway down the table. Her relief had been short-lived. From his lowly position Lucas had an excellent view of the top of the table, unhindered by the large floral centrepieces that had masked some of the other guests from each other, and he had seemed intent on making the best use of his vantage point.

Sitting at the head of the table had another drawback, Victoria had soon discovered. It was a natural focus of attention, and it had seemed that every time she leaned towards Scott she caught someone's eye and was forced to make do with a smiling inanity.

Scott's repressed glee at the situation, and wicked *double entendres*, had eventually become too much for Victoria to bear, and she had whispered desperately, 'I know you must be wondering why I pretended that we hadn't met, but I'm afraid I just panicked——'

'I could tell,' Scott grinned, deftly adjusting his wheelchair so he could lean his elbow on the table and rest his leathery chin in his bony hand, angled away from the person on his other side so that they had at least the illusion of privacy.

The table they sat at was big enough to seat the forty or so guests quite comfortably, and Victoria guessed that it was probably two or three tables pushed together under the snowy white linen tablecloth. So long and wide that it almost filled the room, the table was also unusually low. Like the lift and the extra-wide doorways, the table had been designed to fit the needs of a man in a wheelchair. Victoria already knew that the layout of the rest of the house was user-friendly for a handicapped person—Scott had described it to her in proud detail several days ago.

If only he had been as equally forthcoming about his son, Luke! The way that Scott had grouched about his son—there was no mention of the step-relationship—Victoria had pictured him as a pompous, impatient, bull-headed individual, well-meaning but totally misguided in his relentless filial attentions. Without the surname to warn her, naturally Victoria had not made the connection with David's brilliant young boss!

She would have found it impossible to reconcile the two diametrically opposed images of Lucas Grey if it weren't for Scott's grudging admission that maybe his son did have some cause for his over-concern. Scott's physical and mental health had declined sharply three years earlier when his wife had died after a short illness. He had suffered a deep depression that he was only now shaking off although it was an uphill task to convince his children of the fact he could be trusted to manage his own life once again. They still insisted on employing a 'minder' for Scott and he had just as insistently rejected the invasion of his privacy by driving every one of them away with his sheer bloody-mindedness. When the last one had walked out Scott had determined to conduct his own search for a suitable replacement, hence the air of mystery shrouding the advertisement and his decision to conduct the initial interviews in a park and not reveal his specific address until he was ready to present his new employee to his family.

Victoria had understood, if been a little nervous of, his actions. She knew just how debilitating and ultimately self-defeating misguided kindness could become. When Scott finally informed her that he had set up an interview for her with his son, 'just to show him what he'll be getting for his money' Victoria had agreed without too much trepidation. Although nervous, she had been sure that she could make a good impression as a competent, experienced care-giver, mature beyond her years. That was before she had known that her nine o'clock appointment tomorrow morning was here, with Lucas Grey! Now she knew why the address that David had thrown at her over the phone this evening had sounded vaguely familiar, but at the time she had been in such a panic of nerves that it really hadn't registered.

'I presume this charade means you haven't told your family about your job yet.' Scott knew that she had not been looking forward to the inevitable confrontation that would result.

'I . . . I didn't see the point until after I had seen your son—stepson,' she admitted in feeble defence of her cowardice.

'I don't blame you for putting off the evil hour.' Scott grinned knowingly. 'Your young David has that awful "for-your-own-good" air about him. Bet he's a bit of a stuffed shirt . . .'

Victoria sighed. 'As it happens it's lucky I didn't tell them. I'd hate to have gone through all that upheaval for nothing.'

'Nothing? What do you mean?' Scott demanded in a sharp undertone.

She was taken aback. 'Well, obviously I can't take the job now.'

Scott scowled. 'Why not?'

'Well—I couldn't possibly—I mean, with David and Gabrielle being—well, it makes it all so *awkward* . . .'

'Rubbish! Look, Victoria, I told you how many people I saw. I could look for *another* five weeks and never find someone who even came *close* to suiting me as well as you do. And it suits you, too, remember...close to home, flexible hours, good pay...'

'David would hit the roof——' she began weakly.

'You said he was going to hit the roof whatever job you decided to get. I certainly don't expect you to put me before your family, but if you're going to be independent this is a good place to start. Tell him to mind his own business.'

'I wish it was so simple.'

'It *is* simple. You can't get cold feet on me now—I'm relying on you, Victoria. If you don't come, Luke is going to employ another one of those gin-sodden old battle-axes——'

'I'm sure that's an exaggeration.'

Scott shuddered theatrically. He was a New Zealander, Victoria knew, but marriage to a French Canadian had definitely left its mark. In the course of conversation this evening he had let her know that Lucas and Gabby had been schoolchildren when he had married Renata, their mother, scion of a noble family who could trace their lineage back to the pre-revolution French court.

'If they're not bad-tempered old battle-axes they're weedy-looking male wimps or, worst of the lot, simpering teenagers with an eye to the main chance, bawling all over Luke at the slightest little trouble, making sure they rub their cute little tushes up against all the right places——'

'Scott!' Although he was speaking in a low voice Victoria looked nervously down the table. Sure enough, Lucas Grey's suspicious gaze was still upon them. She hoped he couldn't lip-read!

'Well, it's true,' Scott said unrepentantly. 'Come on, Victoria, we shook on it, you made a commitment——'

'See, I'm a disappointment to you already,' said Victoria, trying to let him down lightly. 'I'm sure you can't still want me...'

'*Still* want you? Victoria, I never *stopped* wanting you!'

There was a loud chink of silverware on china and Victoria realised with cold horror that the general conversation at their end of the table had died just as Scott had spoken, and his words had been clearly audible. At least David was out of earshot...his head was bent smilingly towards Gabrielle. Victoria was glad that *somebody's* problems had been solved!

But Lucas Grey...her eyes clashed bravely again with his and her courage swiftly evaporated at his expression. His dark brows were drawn as taut as his mouth and his eyes were stone-black with what she was sure must be angry distaste. She tried to smile innocently but her dry mouth wouldn't co-operate. Fortunately the rest of the guests were well-bred enough to politely ignore the intriguing titbit that had just been dangled under their noses. Normal conversation was smoothly resumed and Victoria gave up trying to straighten out the tangle with Scott. Instead she concentrated on shifting the food around on her plate so that she appeared to be actually eating.

She had half-expected Scott to turn awkward over her refusal to talk, but instead he switched on a rusty charm as he introduced her around after dinner, making light of the fact that she was David's stepmother so that the usual exclamations of surprise and curiosity were muted. Victoria made a valiant effort to be sociable but couldn't manage it while simultaneously trying to keep a safe distance from Lucas Grey, ignore the pressure of David's silent anxiety that she wasn't enjoying herself, and worry about what Scott's high spirits were going to prompt him to say next.

In the end, to her shame, she was driven to invent a headache to escape. Only slight, but enough to trigger David's latent concern. After he had garaged her car David tucked his jacket unnecessarily around Victoria's shoulders and whisked her off into the night—not quite quickly enough to stop Scott kissing her hand and giving her a slow wink that indicated to her sinking heart that he wasn't yet willing to let the matter rest. She mumbled a hurried goodnight to Lucas's chest and fled...

Victoria let the dishwater drain away and dried her hands on the kitchen towel. All in all it had not been a very edifying experience—her first party in years. When all her stepchildren were living at home Victoria had enjoyed the many spontaneous parties that had erupted, but she had always been conscious of her dual responsibilities as hostess and chaperon. Joshua had never been a great one for going out; he had preferred quiet dinners at home with a few like-minded colleagues. Victoria had no friends of her own age and only recently had she come to realise how isolated her determination to put the family first had made her.

Victoria picked up the morning newspaper and folded it to the Employment listings. It was no use brooding about lost opportunities. She had to create new ones!

Just after half-past nine, as she was drafting an answer to a promising advertisement, the telephone rang and Victoria reached for it with a sigh. It was probably David with instructions about her car. He had told her that he intended to get the local garage to pick it up and give it a thorough going-over before he would let her drive it again.

'You had an appointment with me this morning.'

That thick, smoky voice had haunted her dreams.

'Who is speaking, please?' she asked shakily, to gain time.

'Coward.' The voice was amused. 'Did you really think I wouldn't follow it up, once I knew who you were?'

'Mr Grey?' she said, valiantly keeping up the pretence.

'What amazing powers of deduction you have, Mrs West, and what a busy life you must lead that you can't manage to keep track of all your appointments. I postponed an important meeting for the sake of this mysterious interview and the interviewee can't even bother to turn up!'

She didn't have to see his face to imagine that crooked smile. 'I'm sorry, I—I——'

'Forgot?'

'No, I——'

'Had a better offer?'

'No!' Her soft voice sharpened. 'I just didn't think that—I told Scott I didn't think it was appropriate. I thought he would have cancelled the appointment...'

'He tried to. But he'd sung so many praises about the mystery woman he'd picked up in the personal columns that his sudden about-face was fascinating to say the least——'

'He did not *pick me up*——'

'The way he described you, you were a paragon of virtue. Not at all the sort of person who would let a man down at the last moment. Imagine my relief when I chiselled the truth out of him and discovered the reason for all that instant intimacy between you two last night. It was also nice to know that I wasn't going to be inviting a total stranger to share our lives...'

Why did that sound so *threatening*? 'I'm not letting him down——' Victoria began firmly.

'Good. When can you start?'

Victoria clutched the receiver. 'I can't! I can't work for my son's fiancée's family.' Her tongue stumbled over the ridiculous phrase.

'Why? Isn't it *done* in your social circle?' The mincing words were a soft jab at her inverted snobbery. 'I assure you, we Greys have a very egalitarian view of the world. Besides, the engagement isn't official yet. Gabby still isn't sure she wants to get married at all yet...'

'That only makes things even more awkward.'

'I'm sure you and I are adult enough to rise above such petty considerations...'

Victoria didn't know why he was tormenting her. Surely he wasn't serious?

'Mr Grey, I don't——'

'After all, there's a bigger issue at stake here. I love my father. Until now he's refused to admit that he needs any help at all. I don't think he realised how much my mother used to do for him until she died. He's been almost impossible to live with ever since, but for a while last night, until you left, he was his jaunty old self!'

Victoria felt dreadful, but she knew when her soft heart was being shamelessly played on. She sucked in a shaky breath.

'I'm sorry. You'll have to find someone else. I . . . I have to go now . . . I have a cake in the oven. Goodbye.'

She hung up on him in mid-protest, put a load of shirts and socks and washable trousers into the automatic machine, and sat stubbornly down to finish her letters.

She had sealed one application and was writing the good copy of a second when she heard the familiar thump and rattle of her little car. She smiled quietly to herself. If the garage was returning it so early it meant that it hadn't had to be serviced. She would be sure to point that out to David next time he thought to question her competence as a car-owner. He had never liked the neat yellow second-hand Corolla she had bought after the devastating accident that had changed all their lives, partly because she hadn't asked his advice before her purchase. Mostly, however, his worries had been for her driving such a small, light vehicle in busy traffic, and Victoria was too careful of his feelings to point out that being in a large, heavy, expensive sedan hadn't saved Joshua.

The smug smile froze on her face when she stepped out on to the sunny front porch and saw exactly who it was unfolding himself from the sheepskin-padded front seat.

'Good morning, Victoria. I had a little difficulty finding the house. Did you know you don't have a letterbox?'

The house was down a long, curving double right-of-way, out of sight of the quiet suburban street.

'It's in the hedge. Jason sideswiped it a few days ago and we haven't put it back up yet,' she said numbly. 'What are you doing here?'

He came up the white-painted steps, holding out her car keys. 'David said he was arranging for your car to be delivered home. I told him not to bother, that I'd do it.'

'You've spoken to David...this morning?' Victoria asked hollowly, her fingers wrapping around the keys he dropped into her reluctant palm. Was that why David hadn't called to tell her about her car—because he intended to wait and vent his outrage in person?

'He did most of the talking. Relax, Victoria, I didn't rat on you.' When she didn't respond he said softly, 'Actually, I'd love a cup of tea.'

She was tempted to direct him to the café at the nearby shops but reminded herself that he was David's boss. Besides...she frowned.

'How were you planning to get to work? You have no car.'

He shrugged. 'Taxi. Perhaps I might come inside just long enough to phone for one. Or I could wait out by the gate while you make the call.'

Victoria flushed. After the lavish way he had played a concerned host to her last night he had every right to sound ironic. 'Of course you can come in,' she said, nettled at being put so swiftly in her place.

He mounted the steps. 'Perhaps you might offer me a piece of that cake you were baking when I called,' he murmured.

Victoria's flush deepened.

He paused at the door, looking down at her with laughing brown eyes. 'I hope your headache last night didn't keep you from sleeping.'

'Oh...' Victoria was furious with him for rubbing her nose in her lies, her freckles standing out like peppered shot on her pink face. 'Just go inside!'

'Thank you,' he said, very meekly, holding the door open for her and closing it gently behind them as he followed her closely down the short hallway to the spick and span kitchen.

'The telephone's there.' She pointed to it and moved hurriedly across to the other side of the room, away from his disturbing presence. His dark grey suit jacket was unbuttoned, revealing a pale salmon shirt tucked into the flat waistband of his trousers. Narrow-waisted and lean-hipped, with broad shoulders, his body had an aggressive, top-heavy masculinity. Scott had told her that his son was thirty-two, but it pleased Victoria to decide that the hard angles of his face and body made him look older. In an old pair of Maxine's jeans and a plain white shirt, her thick brown hair bundled into a short pony-tail, she felt at such a sartorial disadvantage that she had to find fault somewhere! His aura of confidence, however, was impossible to fault, and she found herself backing away from his subtle challenge.

'Thank you. And I take my tea black, with sugar,' he added helpfully as she turned around to find something to fiddle with on the empty bench.

At least filling the kettle gave her something to do. Victoria got out two of her best cup-and-saucer sets and willed the water to boil quickly as she heard Lucas give the taxi company her address. When she heard him murmur, 'Shall we say forty-five minutes?' she turned and stared at him accusingly.

Lucas shrugged as he replaced the receiver. 'They're busy,' he offered gravely. 'I'll just have my quick cup of tea and leave. I wouldn't like to hold up whatever it was that you were doing...' His eye fell on the paper lying on the breakfast-bar and one eyebrow slanted pro-vocatively as he noted the penned circles and the neatly addressed envelope lying beside it.

Victoria snatched them up and pushed them into a nearby drawer, her jaw setting as she prepared to fend off another ironic remark. To her surprise Lucas moved over to look out of the window at the flower-filled side garden.

'This looks like a very stately old house from the front. Is it as big as it looks?'

'I'm afraid so.'

He turned around. 'Afraid? Don't you like it?'

'Oh, yes,' Victoria hastened to assure him. 'It's just that a lot of it is wasted space with five bedrooms and only three of us living here. I think there's nothing so melancholy as a house that's only partly lived-in. It really needs a young family to do it justice...'

'If you feel like that, why don't you sell? Or are you only renting?'

'No ... but the house is really David's and it has a lot of happy memories for him. I can understand why he wants to hang on to the place where he was born.'

Another arched eyebrow. 'Literally?'

'Oh, no. But Joshua and Miranda bought it just after they were married ...'

'And he left the house to his son rather than his second wife?'

'David is Joshua's trustee.' Victoria chose her words carefully. 'Josh knew that if anything happened to him, David would look after me ...'

'What if you didn't want to be looked after? What if you wanted to make your own independent decisions. Do you mean he didn't leave you *anything* of your own?'

Victoria stiffened at the hint of criticism. 'He had already given me more than enough. He was a very generous man.' Within the limits of his comfortable income which, with five hungry young mouths to feed, was often under pressure.

'The lounge is just next door; why don't you go through and I'll bring the tea when it's ready?' It was a direction, not a question, and she was relieved when he obeyed. Somehow sharing a kitchen with him seemed even more intimate than sharing a bathroom! She certainly didn't want to treat him with the relaxed casualness of a friend, exchanging confidences over the teacups.

When she carried the tray into the large lounge with its big, old-fashioned but very comfortable roll-armed sofa and chairs, she found Lucas, one hand thrust absently in his pocket, inspecting the array of photographs which decorated the wall beside the exposed brick mantelpiece.

'Is this your husband?'

He was looking at a photograph of a portly, smiling middle-aged man with his arm tucked around a younger, thinner Victoria.

'No. That was my father. That's Josh.'

She pointed to a brawny, dark-haired man holding a huge trout.

'He was a good-looking man,' Lucas murmured abruptly, with a hint of accusation, as if she had deceived him in some way. 'For his age, that is.'

He glanced at her, and her surprise at the sullen truculence of his qualification must have shown, for he added quickly, 'David looks very like him.'

'Yes, all the children are very handsome,' said Victoria steadily, realising with a little sting of acid amusement what had prompted his grudging praise. 'Did you expect him to look old and decrepit? I didn't marry him out of pity. Or for his money. I married him because I *wanted* to...'

'You sound defensive. Have you had to defend your marriage often?'

She turned away to sit down on the sofa and pour the tea, annoyed that he turned the tables again so effortlessly. 'People gossip. The fact that I was much younger and nowhere near Josh's intellectual equal gave them a lot of grist for their mill. Even some of his friends took years to accept that I wasn't going to run off at the drop of a hat with someone my own age...'

'Who's that? His first wife?'

Victoria looked up, her face softening at the sight of the wind-blown blonde. 'Yes, that's Miranda.'

'She was a very beautiful woman.'

'Yes, she was.' She didn't respond to the curiosity in his voice, pushing his tea across the small, low coffee-table, hoping he would take the hint.

He didn't. He came across and sat beside her on the sofa, one arm stretching along the back so that his body inclined towards her, forcing her to acknowledge her own awareness of him. Under the thin shirt she could see a dark shadow and guessed that his chest must be thickly covered with hair. Judging by the amount of silky black hair revealed by the slide of his cuffs about his strong wrists, he would probably be hairy all over. It was a petrifying thought. Victoria sipped her tea, her eyes lowered, desperately trying to think of something to say.

'You've chipped your polish.'

'I beg your pardon?'

He bent close enough for her to scent his male warmth. 'The nail polish on your thumbnail is chipped.'

'That's why I usually don't bother to wear it,' she said, her cup rattling in its saucer as she put it down to check the hand that he had indicated. 'It comes off too quickly when I'm doing housework.'

He took her hand as if he had the perfect right to touch her whenever he wanted to. 'Don't you wear gloves? Your hands are very soft. You must have very sensitive skin.'

His finger slid against her curved palm, tracing up the long crease of her love-line. A tingle shot up her arm and she jerked away, almost upsetting his cup. Hurriedly she picked her own up again and gulped it, burning the inside of her mouth. She began to cough and her eyes blurred with pain.

Gently he took her cup away and put it safely down on the tray with his.

'You're not going to be able to relax, are you, until we get this out in the open?'

'Get what out in the open?' she choked, horrified that he could read her innermost thoughts.

'Look, Dad explained to me how delighted you were with the job he offered you. And he was delighted with you. Having met you I know why.' Victoria felt herself respond helplessly to his frank sincerity, his utter seriousness as he continued gravely, 'Not only do you get on with the old man, but you're obviously a very practical, compassionate sort of person and you have experience at coping with a handicapped person in the home.' His voice gentled as he referred to Steven, but the reference only afforded her a fleeting pain. 'Dad said that you're capable but don't *fuss* ... That was his big objection to the others—that and the fact that live-in help makes him feel claustrophobic—as if he's being "spied" on, or "guarded". So we obviously have to compromise.

'As you probably know Gabby and I travel quite a lot and my workload is pretty intense. Our housekeeper, Iris, comes in every day and usually gets Dad his meals, but she doesn't have time to be company for him as well; nor, frankly, does she have the temperament for it. I must admit when Dad first showed me that ad I was pretty furious, not to mention sceptical about the kind of weirdo who might reply...' His mouth crooked as she bridled visibly. 'But as it turned out I couldn't have chosen better myself. If I offered you more money would it help?'

'Of course not!' The sum that Scott had mentioned had sounded impossibly generous to one who had never earned her living before. 'I...you must have realised that David doesn't know that I've even been *looking* for a job...'

'I can handle David, Victoria. If he's so worried about your status I can make it sound more like a favour than a job, which, in view of your reluctance, it is. Providing, of course, that David is the *real* obstacle we're facing here.'

'What else could there be?' she asked warily, warned by his bland expression.

'Me.' Now the seriousness was leavened by a wry self-derision that was almost as appealing. 'I make you nervous. I'd hate to think that Dad was going to suffer because you feel uncomfortable around me, but I wouldn't be around the house all that much and Dad does have his own separate rooms. I'm sure you could avoid me with very little effort...'

Avoiding him wasn't the problem—*wanting* to was! Victoria wasn't so naïve that she didn't know *why* he made her feel uncomfortable.

He saved her the trouble of finding a face-saving reply by playing his last, trumping card. 'Did Dad tell you that he tried to commit suicide a year ago?'

Victoria's horrified expression gave him his answer.

'I thought not. He's refused to discuss it with anyone, even his doctor. He tried to wash down some pills with a quart of whisky. Neither Gabby nor I were at home that weekend but fortunately I had arranged for Iris to call in on the Saturday to check that he was OK. That was when he hit rock-bottom. He's on the way back up now, but you can see why we're desperate for him to be happy.

'Victoria, he needs you. *I* need you. Won't you please reconsider and at least give us a try? We'd be so very, very grateful. If it doesn't work out there'll be no blame on you, I promise. And whatever happens you'll walk away with a reference fit for a saint!'

CHAPTER FOUR

'I KNOW it's not *good* for him, Mrs Ransome, but what use is good, wholesome food if he doesn't actually *eat* any of it?'

Iris Ransome looked unimpressed by this logic. The clash of pots in the sink expressed her opinion and Victoria sighed as she put the lunch tray down on the highly polished stainless steel bench. She hadn't meant to offend the housekeeper. She had been very careful in the past two weeks *not* to usurp any of the woman's jealously guarded responsibilities. Iris and David would make a good pair, she thought wryly. They both heartily resented her presence in the Grey household and were only constrained from saying so by some nebulous threat of Lucas's.

'I wasn't criticising, Mrs Ransome——'

'Sounded like it to me.' The woman swept around, her soapy hands setting on her broad hips and leaving damp patches on the floral apron. Iris Ransome had a gruff, barking voice and an abrupt manner, her stocky figure and short, basin-cut grey hair adding to the generally military air that had lead Scott to wickedly nickname her 'Sarge'. She ran a tight ship along well-practised lines and didn't like any interference in her routine.

'Well, I wasn't——'

'Got you wrapped around his thumb, hasn't he?' snorted Iris. 'He's a cunning one. One egg a week, that's what his diet sheet says. And no ham!'

'Diet sheet?' Victoria echoed hollowly.

A sour grin. 'You mean he hasn't told you? His doctor has him on a special diet. I knew some things were missing from my refrigerator, but I thought they were for you. Mr Lucas told me you had free rein to help yourself.' She sniffed to show what she thought of that idea.

Victoria was pink. The old devil! No wonder Scott had been so keen to shout her lavish morning or afternoon teas on their daily walks.

'Mr Grey—Lucas—didn't mention——' she began.

'Mr Lucas leaves the meal-planning to me!' snapped Iris.

'Yes, of course,' said Victoria hurriedly.

'After ten years cooking for this family I know exactly what everyone's likes and dislikes are. I don't need telling by the likes of you.'

'No, Sar—er—Mrs Ransome——'

Iris didn't look at all dismayed by her slip. If anything she looked gratified as she turned back to her dishes. 'Well, now you know. Diet sheet is on the fridge, for future reference. And no point your keeping on bringing your own packed lunch and putting extra temptation his way. You may as well eat my cooking, too.'

Mollified by that magnificent concession, Victoria still felt chastened as she slunk out into the hall. And she had thought she was learning to handle Scott quite well!

As she moved past the lift towards the cluster of rooms that passed as Scott's 'separate apartment' a voice stopped her in her tracks.

'Survived another military skirmish, Victoria?'

If she'd been still carrying the tray she would have dropped it. As it was she whirled around against the wall, her heart thundering.

Lucas Grey was standing just behind her. For a big man he moved very quietly.

'You're in Bonn!' protested Victoria, when she got her breath under control.

'Clever me,' murmured Lucas, his mouth curving. 'Am I just an illusion, do you think?' He reached to brush his fingers along her collarbone, exposed by the demure cotton dress that she felt was suitable for her job.

'You're supposed to be there for a week. You left this morning.' The tiny, casual caress stung her guilty imagination. He had kept out of her way, as promised, and yet she found his elusiveness a double-edged sword. He was so...unexpected. Even when safely out of the country, he never seemed to be completely *gone*...

'One of my department heads went instead.'

From what Victoria had heard, the Bonn conference was a very important one, and Lucas rarely delegated important responsibilities. She eyed him warily.

'He needed the experience,' he added smoothly. 'How are you and Iris getting on?'

She was immediately on the defensive. 'Has she been complaining about me?'

'Iris complains about everything and everyone, but she has a good heart. It'll take her time to get used to having someone else constantly underfoot.'

Victoria bristled. 'I'm not underfoot. Scott and I go out for at least a couple of hours every day.'

'I know, I meant that she takes a while to adjust to new situations,' he gentled. 'Would you like to come in and look at my new study?' He indicated the half-open door beside him, the room that she'd slipped into to remove her tights that first night. She shied off nervously at the memory.

'Scott is just setting up the chess-board——'

'Good, you have time, then. Besides, I think you and I need to have a little talk.'

The most ominous words in the English language, decided Victoria nervously as she walked past him into the large white room.

'Oh!'

It had been totally transformed since she had last been inside. It was still all white, but now the black leather chair had been joined by banks of high-tech equipment that softly hummed and ticked in the quiet room. Victoria recognised none of the electronic wizardry— except for the small, conventional computer on the white desk, a top-of-the-line brand.

'Like it?'

She nodded. The black and white starkness of the Picasso prints perfectly complemented the clean, hard monochrome lines of the machines.

'I . . . I don't understand any of it, but it looks very impressive,' said Victoria faintly. 'What does it all do?'

She might as well have waved a magic wand with her innocent question.

'I'm opening up a new avenue of research...' His eyes glittered with enthusiasm as he took her around the room, introducing her to each item with a grave affection that implied that the lumps of plastic and metal were living entities. Perhaps to him they were. Victoria nodded and tried hard to look intelligent and not stare at him as he plunged deeper and deeper into the esoteric field of his endeavours. He suddenly reminded her of Jason—utterly absorbed in his subject, blithely convinced that no one could fail to share his boyish intellectual excitement. She smiled at the comparison.

'Have I said something funny?'

Victoria floundered. She couldn't say anything intelligent about his work, since she still wasn't sure exactly what it entailed; she had been listening to his eager tone of voice rather than the substance of his words.

'I—you're very passionate about your work——'

Passionate was very definitely the wrong word to use. She blushed that he might think it was a Freudian slip and the slight remaining glaze of self-absorption vanished from his eyes.

'I'm very passionate about a lot of things, Victoria,' he murmured, straight-faced. 'And reckless, when inspiration strikes. Are you?'

'Reckless?' she said, purposely misunderstanding him. 'Never. What was it you wanted to talk to me about?'

'Never? You're very young to be using that word.' He hitched a hip on the white desk and gestured towards the soft leather chair at his knee. 'Sit down.' When Victoria remained stiffly standing he said, irresistibly, 'Please?'

She sat, folding her hands in her lap so that she wouldn't fidget. She looked at him calmly and he looked back.

'Verdigris.'

'I beg your pardon?'

'The colour of your eyes—in certain lights, in certain moods, it's the same as the green rust you get on exposed copper.'

'Is that a compliment, or a scientific evaluation?' asked Victoria, a sudden tightness in her chest.

He smiled. 'You decide. How have you settled in so far?'

'Fine.'

'Any problems?'

'No,' she said firmly.

'And would you tell me if there were?'

She didn't answer immediately and his eyes narrowed.

'You will admit that, as your employer, I do have a right to ask *some* questions——'

'But Scott's rights have to come first. I work with and for him and he needs to be able to trust my loyalty. I'll never gain his respect or confidence if I don't give him mine first.'

He gave her a hard look. 'That's not the way I intended our arrangement to work.'

'I'm sorry.'

His frown smoothed to a quizzical ruffle. 'No, you're not. You enjoy thwarting me, don't you, Victoria? You think it gives you an edge.'

An edge over what?' she wanted to ask, but didn't dare.

'You know *why* it's important to me to know what state of mind he's in——' Lucas said in a softly cajoling voice that stiffened her resolve.

'Yes. I fully appreciate your concern,' she said coolly. 'If anything occurs that I think you need to know, of course I'll discuss it with you.'

'Thank you——' his swift assumption of victory faltered '—I *think*. Anything *you* think I need to know? Doesn't that put us right back where we started?'

'Where else did you expect us to be?' asked Victoria serenely.

He folded his arms over his chest, settling more securely on to the desk as he studied her gentle air of pliant meekness. 'I'm not sure. I *thought* I was getting my own way.'

'And aren't you?'

He looked down at his polished shoes, considering. He had thick lashes for a man, thought Victoria, to go with those thick brows. His open-necked maroon shirt also showed the springy soft black hair of his chest, as luxuriant as she had imagined it to be. He was wearing shabby white jeans, tight across the hips. She had never seen him casually dressed before; he had always worn suits when dashing off to his various meetings. In formal clothes he had been quite intimidating enough and it was annoying to realise that his flagrant masculinity was even more threatening for its casual unconsciousness. He looked up and caught her in the act of studying his male anatomy. This time she refused to blush.

'I think perhaps I'm getting what I *deserve*,' he murmured cryptically. 'Which is not quite the same thing. I suppose what I'm really trying to find out, Victoria, is whether you're happy.'

'Well, Mrs Ransome is so ultra-efficient that really there's not a great deal of housework to do, but Scott certainly enjoys having company,' she said, not quite sure what he was getting at. 'I think one of his problems is boredom. He's starting to talk about rejoining the Archery Club, though...' Scott had told her it had been a sport he had taken up after his accident, to be abandoned along with all his other outside interests and friends when his wife died.

'I asked about you. Do you think *you're* going to like it here?'

'Yes.' Though Scott could be very self-willed and demanding she liked him, and admired him. He had picked himself up after a devastating blow, shaken off his self-pity, and was forging a new life out of the old pain.

'Is David still making things difficult at home?'

'A little,' she hedged. 'But you don't have to worry——'

'I'm not. I've just seen you in action...a sweet and gentle juggernaut. I thought I might have to protect you from Scott. Now I see the reverse might be true!'

He meant to tease, but she refused to rise to the bait. She was determined to keep a proper and respectful distance as befitted her position.

'Did you know it's Dad's birthday next month?'

'No.' Victoria was becoming used to the way his mind was constantly leap-frogging from one subject to another.

'My mother always used to make a big thing of family birthdays.' Lucas's voice unconsciously softened when he spoke of his mother, she noticed. Scott rarely mentioned his late wife and there were no photographs of her on display—Victoria found herself intensely curious. 'She liked to create surprises for us all, and that's what I'd like to do for Dad. For the last few years he wouldn't let us celebrate his birthday at all...'

'Do you think that's wise—to spring something on him like that?' Victoria's expression revealed her own dislike of surprises.

'Oh, I didn't mean a party. I meant his present. I'd like it to make up for the three years we didn't dare get him one...'

'What have you got in mind?' asked Victoria cautiously.

'Well, considering how relentlessly fit he used to be——'

'Victoria? Victoria? Where are you? I thought you said you wanted to play white? Victoria!' Scott's voice was querulous with irritation as it pierced the hallway. The half-open door to the office was nudged wider with a wheel, making Victoria appreciate the padded protective strips that adorned the internal doors in the house.

'So there you are! What's going on?' His mouth pinched with suspicion. 'Delivering your report, Victoria?'

'Refusing to deliver it, more accurately, Dad,' said Lucas drily. 'She's informed me that you're her master, not me.'

Scott Sinclair grunted his satisfaction. 'Thought she'd be a pushover for your charm, huh? I could have told you it was a waste of time. Why do you think I chose her? I knew she had a sensible head on her shoulders. I told her all about those little floozies who kept tripping over your feet...'

'I didn't give them any encouragement,' Lucas growled, and Victoria was amused to notice a slight change in his colour.

'It must be tiresome to be irresistible to women,' she said kindly, daring to tease now that Scott was there to protect her.

'Girls,' he corrected drily. 'If I were irresistible to women you and I would be in bed by now.'

'Lucas!' To Victoria's chagrin Scott didn't share her outraged reaction. He coughed a sharp laugh, thumping the arm of his chair. He wasn't using the electronic version that Lucas had personally designed for him, otherwise he might have shot out of the room in reverse.

'You started it,' Lucas said unrepentantly. 'You know what Shakespeare said: "Tempt not a desperate man..."'

'That hardly applies in this case!' said Victoria tartly.

'How do you know how desperate I am?' he murmured. 'You never come close enough to find out.'

'Are we going to play chess or what?'

'Or what,' said Lucas, and slanted a grin at Victoria's prim expression. 'She'll join you in a few moments, Dad. We just need another word.'

'About what?'

'None of your business, old man.'

'What's all this stuff doing in here?' Scott changed tactics. 'It looks like a laboratory.'

'It is, in a way. Just something I'm tinkering with at work...'

'So what's it doing here?'

'I'm going to be working from home for a time. For security reasons.'

'This is the first I've heard of it,' frowned Scott while Victoria looked on, appalled. Lucas was going to be around all the *time*? 'Who's going to run the business while you're puttering around here?'

'Gabby.'

'Gabby?' Scott looked thoughtful.

'It's always been on the cards that she'll take over administration one day and leave me free to concentrate on the technical side. I wouldn't be giving her this chance, Dad, if I didn't think she was ready for it.'

'You really think she is?'

Lucas shrugged. 'There's only one way to find out. And at least this way her confidence won't be devastated if she can't cut it. If she knows I'm only on temporary leave she'll look on it as a great opportunity to prove her abilities rather than a make-or-break test. She'll know I'm here to give her advice and yet I won't be hovering at her shoulder waiting for her to make a mistake.'

'Mmm, you could be right.'

Victoria, still coping with her shock, was nevertheless impressed by Lucas's perception of Gabrielle's character. She had seen enough of the young woman to know that she was serious in her desire to entrench herself in the family business but that her personality was more volatile, less ruthlessly confident than that of her brother. She had been frankly friendly towards Victoria, laughing off David's 'obtuseness' as she called it. She had also pumped her unmercifully for anecdotes about his youth—a sure sign, Victoria mused, that she was besotted, for by all accounts David had been a boringly well-behaved boy!

'Now, if you don't mind, Dad...?' Luke raised his eyebrows expectantly and Scott backed his chair out of the room, muttering under his breath. Victoria knew she would be in for an interrogation later. For too long Scott had been uninterested in events around him. He was making up for it with a vengeance!

'You're really going to be working at home. For how long?' Victoria couldn't stop herself asking.

'I don't know. Is it a problem?'

'Well, if you're going to be here all the time, perhaps my job is redundant...'

Lucas laughed. 'You haven't seen me at work. I'm on a different planet. You don't need to worry that you'll be tripping over my feet, Victoria. You won't even notice I'm here.'

She looked at him in disbelief. 'This is all rather sudden, isn't it?'

'Not at all,' he lied without a blink, adding more truthfully, 'I've been planning to ease Gabby into the helm for some time. I know she's eager for responsibility, but I wanted to make sure she was secure in her personal as well as professional life before I let her off the leading reins.'

Victoria opened her mouth to ask him whether he was referring to David but he continued seamlessly, 'Now, much as I'd love to continue this cosy chat, we did agree that your first loyalty is to my father, so we'd better not keep him waiting.'

Victoria shut her mouth with a snap and he grinned. 'You can pester me about my private life tomorrow afternoon, when we go shopping.'

'Shopping?'

'For Scott's present. I need your advice.'

'Why mine? What about Gabrielle?'

'Gabby has too much on her plate already.'

'But it's not until next month——'

'We'll need all that time and more to do what I want to do.'

'Oh, I see, you've already made up your mind. I'm just along for the ride.'

He slanted a look at her under half-closed lids, extremely tempted, but thought better of it. 'I would value your advice, Victoria,' he said gravely. 'Please? It has to be right for him. I don't want him going off at the deep end with memories of other birthdays...'

He was doing it again. He must know how it made her feel, to have this big, hard, aggressive male softly begging her for favours in that wistful, smoky voice. As if he was kneeling at her feet rather than towering domi-

nantly over her. She could feel her feet sinking, along
with her resistance, into the thick carpet as she rose unsteadily in an attempt to assert herself.

'I would really deem it an excellent favour,' he said
meekly, taking her hand.

She snatched it feverishly away. 'Don't overdo it,
Lucas.'

'I think I already did.' His eyes glinted at her, en-
joining her to laugh at the little game they were playing.
'You will do it, won't you? For Scott's sake?'

'Yes, all right,' she said aware that her reluctance held
a certain forbidden excitement. A tiny acid drop of guilt
fell on her heart, burning, hurting. She closed her eyes
briefly.

'Victoria?' His playfulness fell away like a cloak, his
voice dark and gentle yet still exerting a force of will.
'If you really object I won't make you. But I think it
could be fun...'

That was what she was afraid of. She made one last
feeble attempt to deny herself. 'I can't do it after three
o'clock.' The little acid drop burnt quietly deeper. 'I—
'

'I didn't intend that you should use up your own
valuable time,' he said swiftly. 'I'll just ask Scott if I
can "borrow" you for an experiment tomorrow. I'm sure
he won't mind giving you a free hour or two. Now run
along and let me get on with my work...' For all the
world as if she had been the one pestering him!

'Well, as you can see, Mrs Grey, we have a wide range
of——'

'Mrs West.'

'I beg your pardon?'

Victoria gritted her teeth. 'My name is Mrs West. I
am *not* this man's wife.'

'This man' stood there smiling lazily as the salesman
looked uncertainly from one to the other. 'She's very
independent,' he drawled. 'She refuses to make an honest
man of me.'

'Nothing will *ever* make you honest, Lucas Grey,' said Victoria, her soft voice sharp with embarrassment. 'In fact marriage is only likely to compound the problem!'

'Not if you married me, darling. I'd be faithful until the day I died,' said Lucas, laying a hand over his wicked heart.

'Which would be shortly after the wedding!' Victoria snapped. She turned her back on him and impaled the salesman with a stern stare. 'You realise that this is for a disabled man? He's fit but he has virtually no lateral hip movement, or elasticity in his joints.'

'Yes, your hu—er—Mr Grey explained.' The salesman gulped, wondering what such a prim-mouthed, freckle-faced little lady could have done to have that handsome brute hustling her the way he did. She must be dynamite in bed. 'This particular item is designed to build upper-body strength. Why, even you could use it. Here, have a try...'

Actually, apart from the freckles she wasn't bad, and her skin felt soft through the thin blouse. She had good legs and a small waist and breasts that would make a nice handful if a man felt inclined to unbutton that up-tight blouse and...

'Forget it!' The harsh growl jolted him out of his pleasant fantasy.

'Huh?' The precious couple of seconds it took him to recover cost the salesman his commission. 'Hey—Mr Grey—you haven't let me explain the terms——!'

'Lucas! Lucas, let go of my arm. What are you doing? We hadn't even checked out the equipment!' protested Victoria in exasperation as she was dragged out of the large department store.

'Oh, equipment has been checked out, all right, but it wasn't of the hardware kind. What that guy wanted you to do on the bench press certainly wasn't anything to do with lifting weights!'

'What *are* you talking about?' Victoria finally got her elbow out of his grasp as they stood on the curb.

Lucas threw up an imperious hand and a taxi appeared like magic. He thrust her inside.

'Are you so immune to men leering down your blouse that you didn't notice the drool stains?'

Victoria stared at him as if he was mad. 'There's no *down* to look; my blouse is buttoned right up to the neck!' she pointed out, lifting her chin from the demure pink ruffle that edged her stand-up collar.

'You mean you weren't offended?' he rasped, throwing the address of another store to the driver before he sat back and watched Victoria twitch her demure skirt back into place after her hasty entrance into the car.

'At what?' she was honestly bewildered.

'He was touching you.'

'He just took my arm to show me what to do. If anyone was leering it was you.'

'He was a sleazeball. These guys put on a few muscles and think it makes them studs. Or they're gay——'

'Well he can't have been leering at me then, can he? Maybe he was drooling over *you*. Your cleavage is more plunging than mine, and your jeans are positively indecent!'

'They fit perfectly. At least denim is thicker than tissue paper. That blouse is practically see-through.'

'It is not!'

'You're wearing a white cotton bra with a little bit of lace around the top of the cup.'

'Lucas!' She clutched her handbag to her breasts, her face brilliant as she caught the taxi driver's muffled chuckle.

Her dismay seemed to improve his surly temper.

'You didn't even notice him, did you?'

'No, I didn't,' she admitted with the dignity of a born lady.

'Don't notice much, do you?'

'Not when you're around!' She heard him draw a quick breath and realised what she had said. 'I mean, you're so big!'

He raised an eyebrow.

'When are we going to buy some of this gymnastic equipment, Lucas?' she said severely. 'We must have looked at every brand there is and still you haven't made a decision. I thought it was going to be one afternoon... and this is the second time in a week. Scott's beginning to get suspicious and I don't blame him. So far I don't see why you need me with you at all,' she tacked on darkly, 'except to have somebody to embarrass!'

'But you embarrass so exquisitely!'

'Lucas——!'

'All right, all right. We'll go to lunch and draw up a list and come up with a plan to renovate the old pool-house without Scott finding out what's going on. OK?'

'No. I can't——' Lunch was the thin end of the wedge as far as she was concerned. 'Scott is expecting me back——'

'No, he's not,' said Lucas calmly, and leaned forward to change his order to the driver. 'I told him I'd need you a bit longer today.'

Victoria was still protesting as the doorman at a very chic and fashionable Auckland restaurant was assisting her from the taxi with his gloved hand.

'Don't fuss, Victoria,' Lucas said as he paid the driver and tipped the doorman.

'He touched me, didn't you notice?' she said nastily.

'I noticed he was old enough to be your grandfather.'

'I like older men.' She was behaving childishly but she couldn't help it. 'They certainly have more manners!'

He opened the door of the restaurant with exaggerated politeness and Victoria sailed past him, her freckled nose in the air. Her haughty indifference couldn't last long, however, and when they were seated at the table she was absorbed in her surroundings. The restaurant was in a renovated ferry building on Auckland's waterfront and they were seated on a small enclosed balcony that overlooked the wharf where a number of tall ships were tied up, training vessels for aspiring young sailors or charter groups.

'Have you been here before?'

Victoria shook her head, admiring the modern décor that blended so well with the old building that housed it, drinking in the atmosphere with a repressed eagerness that made him curious.

'There are quite a number of good restaurants along the waterfront these days...' He named one or two others and when Victoria said she hadn't heard of them he asked her for her own favourites. Victoria looked blank.

'Well, the one you've been to most recently, then.'

Victoria fidgeted with her menu. 'I...I don't remember. It was a while ago...'

He looked at her quietly for a moment as the waiter came to take their order. 'What would you like to eat?'

She opened her menu. It was very spare and elegant, and in French. 'I'm really not very hungry, just something light will do,' she said, to give herself time to find something that sounded vaguely familiar and easily pronounceable. She was conscious of the waiter standing expectantly there, as smugly chic as the restaurant itself, and she didn't want to embarrass Lucas by flaunting her ignorance.

'The chef here has a very light touch,' said Lucas, watching her eyes run anxiously over the pages. 'If you're feeling a little adventurous I could recommend something that I think you'd like.'

'That would be nice,' she said, uncertainly grasping the lifeline. The word 'adventurous' wasn't in her vocabulary.

He read out the name of the dish from the menu and then proceeded to describe in his own words how it was made, and with what ingredients, grinning as her brow wrinkled.

'I know it sounds odd, lamb and hard-boiled eggs and anchovies, but it's based on a very famous seventeenth-century French recipe inspired by the Condé family and it's probably not something you'd ever try at home. Trust me.'

In the circumstances she had little choice. She nodded, reluctantly, and sipped at the iced water the waiter poured before he withdrew.

'It's truly delicious, Victoria. And much more exciting than an omelette.'

So he knew. She met his eyes and saw the gentle amusement there, and appreciated the way he had skilfully preserved her dignity even while he was backing her into a corner. 'I always hated French at school,' she admitted ruefully. 'I'm afraid I didn't pay much attention. My teachers said I was a dreamer but that was really just a kind way of saying I was a failure. We lived in a very small country community, and being the daughter of a vicar and of an historian I was expected to be both obedient *and* clever. I could manage the one, but not the other,' she added with a faintly rueful resignation.

'A vicar's daughter? I've heard of them, of course, but I don't think I've actually ever met one before,' said Luke in amusement. 'It explains a lot...'

'Like what?' Now there were some oddly shaped, garlicky rolls delivered to the table and Victoria's hand hovered over the array of knives on the table until she saw Lucas deftly break his open with his fingers. She followed suit and filled her mouth with the crunchy-soft roll.

'Your gentle spirit...the definite leaning towards self-sacrificing martyrdom——'

'I don't consider it self-sacrificing to be considerate of others.'

'At the expense of yourself? If I hadn't insisted, you would have let David's opinion do you out of a job you very much wanted.'

She managed to divert him by talking determinedly about the different types of fitness equipment they had just seen until Lucas capitulated and obediently made a list of their choices. He sketched a plan of the poolhouse on a white linen napkin and during the meal, which was as delicious as he had promised, managed to skilfully sidetrack her into revealing a little more about her quiet aspirations. Halfway through coffee Victoria stiffened and went pale.

'Victoria? What's the matter?'

'It's David. He and Gabrielle have just walked in. Don't look!' It was too late. 'Oh, God, they're going to see us!' Victoria was almost sliding under the table as the other couple were shown to a nearby table, her freckles standing out on her milk-white face.

'Calm down, Victoria. We're having lunch together, that's all. There's nothing to feel guilty about. After all, it's what they're doing.'

'Yes, but *they're* almost engaged!' Victoria wished she still had the incomprehensible menu to hide behind.

'You think a man and woman dining together in a public restaurant are automatically assumed to be intimately involved?' Lucas said incredulously. 'Victoria, this is the twentieth century. I can't believe that even a country vicar's daughter is *that* far behind the times!'

'Oh, he's seen us.' Victoria's complexion went from pale to flushed in the space of a heartbeat. 'I knew I shouldn't have come——'

'Victoria, relax. You haven't done anything wrong.' Lucas captured her fluttering hand and pressed firmly down on the tablecloth.

But she had, and she didn't need David's piercingly accusing gaze to tell her.

'What David thinks is his problem. You don't have to explain anything if you don't want to——'

'He's coming over,' whispered Victoria miserably.

'Good. I'd like a word with him.' Lucas swivelled around in his chair and gave his sister a grin before greeting David with a cool smile.

'Hello, David, did you come over to ask us to join you? I'm afraid we've just eaten.'

David was staring at the clasped hands on the tablecloth. Victoria quickly snatched her hand back and tucked it in her lap, knowing she was only making things worse by acting guilty but unable to stop herself. She *was* guilty.

'Aren't you supposed to be working today, Tory?' David's deep voice was rough and surly.

Now she felt like a truant child. 'I am.'

David's eyebrows rose, reminding her so much of Joshua that Victoria felt doubly condemned.

'Victoria has been looking at home-gym equipment with me. Didn't Gabby tell you—we're equipping a gym for Scott for his birthday?'

David flung a brief glance of annoyance back at his fiancée, who smiled and innocently waved. 'No, she didn't.'

'I wonder why,' murmured Lucas, and David shifted uneasily. His bull-headed resistance to his stepmother's job was as implacable as it was indefensible. He couldn't provide an explanation without baring his soul, and Victoria knew his pride would never allow him to do that, especially to a man he had always so admired. Now his admiration was mixed with a deep, contradictory resentment, which only added to his internal confusion.

'Victoria is providing me with some helpful advice on the sly. She's quite knowledgeable on the subject. She tells me she researched quite a bit about physical therapy for the disabled while she was caring for Steven.'

David's glance sharpened and Victoria clenched her hands beneath the concealing folds of the tablecloth. Talking about Steven was evidently considered another betrayal, not because there was anything to hide, but because David knew how reticent Victoria usually was with strangers. How could she explain to him that to remain strangers one needed the co-operation of both parties?

'I've been dragging her around various stores putting her knowledge to good use and, since she wouldn't accept any compensation, I felt the least I could do was offer her lunch,' said Lucas easily. 'Particularly as she said she doesn't get the chance to get out much.'

He made it sound as if Victoria had complained and she opened her mouth to tell David that Lucas was only making an assumption, but David was already reacting badly to the hint of criticism. 'Tory only has to ask Jason or me if she wants to go out,' he said stiffly.

'And does she?' asked Lucas quietly. It didn't seem to occur to David that Victoria might wish to go out with a man who was not a member of her family, he noted curiously.

'Well, no, but that's because...well, she's a homebody. I mean, she likes a peaceful life, don't you, Tory?'

It was a rhetorical question, and anyway Victoria couldn't tell her stepson that sometimes she longed to kick over the traces and celebrate the fact that she was young and *alive*, albeit living a kind of fragile half-life that each day demanded more of her strength and energy to endure. Her job was supposed to be providing an outlet for her understandable frustrations; instead it seemed to be creating new ones! Her eyes darkened with a hint of rebellion as she murmured something innocuous. David seemed satisfied but Lucas was more perceptive. When their meal arrived and her stepson had returned reluctantly to his own table, Lucas said, 'I know you're fiercely loyal, Victoria, but his attitude borders on the obsessive. Is there anything I should know that you're not telling me?'

Anything? Everything! 'In what way?'

'My sister is on the verge of getting engaged to him,' he said drily. 'I've had to rescue her two or three times before from the consequences of a hasty infatuation. I'd hate to think that she's on the verge of another mistake.'

'She's not. David is just——'

'Jealous.' Lucas confirmed his opinion with a nod. 'He's never seen you with a man before, and it's hitting home that you no longer belong exclusively to the West family. He obviously suffered very much when his father died. Now he has to face the fact all over again that his father *isn't* coming back.'

'I—what do you mean?' Victoria's vision darkened with shock.

'I'm right, aren't I? I only have to look at your face to see it.' Lucas said with a quiet triumph. 'Since his father died you haven't even looked at another man, let alone gone out with one. You've cushioned the impact of his loss on the family by allowing them to set you up as a kind of living memorial, but now it's not enough for you, and David senses that, senses the restlessness and is afraid of it—and for you, too, no doubt. I don't blame him. I suspect you're a babe in the woods when it comes to man-woman relationships. You were married and a mother before you had the chance to experiment the way most teenagers do. With your tender heart you're vulnerable enough to fall for the first slick operator to make a play for you.

'What you need, Victoria, is a little practice before you launch yourself properly out into the big, bad world!'

CHAPTER FIVE

IF ONLY she hadn't lost her head. If only she had treated his uncomfortably perceptive comments lightly, as a joke. But she had panicked. As usual she had let her own guilty awareness trap her into making a fool of herself.

Victoria pressed her hot forehead against the cool pane of glass she had just cleaned, still embarrassed at the way she had almost run out of the restaurant to get away from her tormentor. Of course, she hadn't succeeded. Even more humiliating was Lucas's ensuing kindness. All the way home in the taxi he had chatted easily about a variety of safe subjects, as if she hadn't practically accused him of being a vile and conscienceless seducer of innocent widows and orphans. Well, she hadn't actually *said* those things, but her outraged incoherence had probably drawn him a very eloquent picture. All he had done was flirt a little, probably out of sheer habit; her sordid mind had done the rest!

Fortunately Lucas gave her breathing-space to get things back into sensible proportion. Back at the house he had disappeared into his study for the several days, not even emerging for meals. Victoria didn't flatter herself that it was her fault, for Scott told her that it was Lucas's spectacular single-mindedness that had made him such a success in his field.

'A lot of men have his brains, but not his ability to focus his brilliance to the exclusion of everything else. He lets a problem turn over in his mind for hours, days, weeks even, before he's ready to tackle it physically; then there's no stopping him,' Scott had said one morning while trouncing her at chess. 'Other people explore all reasonable possibilities, but Luke likes the challenge of the *un*reasonable. His methods are intuitive and often offbeat, but they generally work. Most of Computel's international reputation for innovation over the past few years can be laid at Luke's door.'

'You're as proud of him as if he were your own son, aren't you?' Victoria had murmured, donating a knight to her stricken conscience. And she had imagined that this extraordinary intuitive genius was interested in her ordinary, plodding self!

'As far as I'm concerned he is my son, just as Gabby is my daughter. That *****' he used an expressive French word that Victoria suspected was obscene '—Renata married didn't deserve the title of father. He didn't give a damn for his children until he realised he could use them to stop her getting a divorce. He turned her family against her and isolated and abused her for all the years it took him to run through her inheritance. He kept her from me as long as he could, out of sheer spite, and then sold his children like cattle when the well ran dry.'

Shocked at the revelation, Victoria was also concerned at the mottled colour of Scott's face, but she knew that bottling up his bitterness could do worse damage. 'Scott——'

His mouth twisted at her gentle concern. 'I'm all right. I'm not going to slit my throat over the past. It's done. I accept that. It just galls me to think he's still out there somewhere enjoying life, while Renata is——' He swallowed, the thin wrinkled throat working. 'We were in love for twenty years and only six of those we had together because of him. Dammit, it should have been more!'

'I know what you mean.' It seemed that everyone that Victoria loved was taken away. And yet she couldn't prevent herself from loving. It was her nature.

'I guess my best revenge is Luke and Gabby,' Scott had gone on with grim satisfaction. 'Lennox Grey was one cold son of a bitch, and if he'd bothered at all with his children other than as a weapon he could have had a devastating effect on their personalities. Thank God that, although Luke is physically very like his father, in personality he's very like Renata—bright and passionate, intense and tenacious. I wish I had his unquenchable spirit. When I lost interest in everything after Renata died Lucas said that I was giving that bastard the ultimate victory, and he was right. I swore then that I'd live to hold his grandchildren in my arms and call them *mine*!'

As a motivation for life it wasn't exactly pure, but it was definitely powerful, Victoria thought. How clever and cunning of Lucas to choose just the right one to spark his stepfather back to life.

Victoria shivered and drew back from the cool window-pane. He was clever and cunning and yet also apparently deeply sensitive. Passionate. Intense. Tenacious. A complex mixture she couldn't hope to understand.

When Lucas had finally resurfaced from his reequipped study he had given no sign that he even remembered the awkwardness of their lunch together. To make up for her unflattering suspicions about him Victoria had made a sincere effort to overcome her shyness and respond to his casualness with equally calm and friendly courtesy, but it had not been easy.

The plans for the gym had progressed at a startling speed which Victoria was beginning to discover was Lucas's usual pace. After only a week he had demanded her opinion of the draughtsman's plan and consulted physical therapy experts on the layout of the equipment...this time bringing them to the house rather than unnerving Victoria by inviting her out with him. A builder was engaged and, since the weather had turned chilly and Scott had carried out his intention to take up archery again, it hadn't been difficult to keep him away from the pool at first. But now the sun was out again and she was having to resort to subterfuge.

'What's so fascinating out there?'

Victoria was horrified to find she was staring blankly out of the window at a man carrying a section of a sauna around the corner of the house. She hastily swung around to face Scott.

'Nothing.'

'You were staring at nothing for an awfully long time.'

Victoria went hot. 'I was just thinking.'

'About going for a dip?' On warm days, before the secret renovations had started, Victoria had joined him in his former daily workouts, wearing a demure black one-piece that Lucas seemed to find amusing. If she had known what the amusement had concealed she would have bundled up like an Eskimo. What Victoria had happily bought for its modest colour and cut was deliciously sexy when wet, loving every dip and curve of her body like a shrink-wrapped second skin. Her own provided a startling contrast, freckles smothering creamy skin that rejected all attempts at tanning. She wasn't a very good swimmer, which was fortunate because Scott was grimly competitive, and would have responded to challenge by pushing himself beyond his capabilities. Lucas, whose study overlooked the pool, had got into the habit of strolling out just in time to help her assist his stepfather from the pool and Victoria had appreciated his consideration. For all his physical frailty, Scott was big-boned and quite a solid weight for her small frame to support. Focusing on him, she never noticed that while Lucas's strong hands were assisting Scott his eyes were lazily enjoying the sheen the wetness imparted to her freckled curves, and the innocently natural response of her breasts to the chill freshness of the air after the warmth of the solar-heated water. Her nipples became full and pointed, stretching the thin black fabric between the taut peaks. It took very little effort for Lucas to imagine himself peeling down that black skin to reveal her nakedness, soft, round, lavishly freckled breasts crowned with chilled rose nipples that he would warm to velvety hardness with his tongue... He was usually deep in the grip of a suffocatingly erotic fantasy by the time Scott was back in his chair and Victoria turned to give Lucas the sweet, shyly unaware smile of thanks that always slammed the lid on his criminal libido. The walk back to his study was invariably a long one, every step a sweetly tearing agony to his aching loins, apt punishment, he accepted wryly, for his self-induced state of arousal.

'The pool people haven't been to check the water yet,' Victoria said, remembering to keep her lies straight.

'Yes, they have,' Scott disconcerted her by replying. 'I called them and asked. They said they didn't even have a record of the complaint. They sent a guy over and he came in and said there was nothing wrong with the PH balance.'

'Oh. M-maybe Lucas made a mistake when he tested it...'

'Lucas? Lucas was practically *born* in a laboratory!' Scott scoffed at the suggestion. 'There's something going on, isn't there? Some reason why I shouldn't swim? Something the doctor has told you——'

'No.' But her eyes skittered away from his and he pounced with sly cunning.

'You hate lying to a crippled old man, don't you, Tory? It must be something really terrible if you think it has to be hidden from me...'

Aghast, she hurried to reassure him. 'It's nothing terrible, I promise you——'

'So there *is* a secret!' he crowed triumphantly.

'Scott——' Even dishonesty in a good cause made her uncomfortable, but Luke would never forgive her if she spoiled his surprise.

'Isn't there?'

She knew he could be as tenacious as his son. 'Yes,' she admitted miserably, 'but it's nothing for you to worry about, Scott, truly.'

'Is it the reason you've been busily keeping me out of the back yard?'

Victoria picked up her window-cleaning equipment and moved to a window safely overlooking a blanket profusion of flowering shrubs.

'Does it have anything to do with my birthday coming up?' he persisted, sounding pleased rather than perturbed, and Victoria's last doubts about the wisdom of Lucas's actions vanished. 'I could make you tell me, you know. I happen to remember you saying that you're ticklish...'

Victoria tried to twist around but it was too late, his wheelchair had her hemmed in and the feather duster she had left on the sideboard was skittering across the backs of her knees.

'Don't, Scott——' Her voice brimmed with uncertain laughter.

'Are you going to confess?'

'Scott, I am *not* going to tell you anything else,' Victoria said as sternly as her giggles would allow, trying to dodge the teasing duster. 'And you're not to try and find out. Promise?'

He liked to hear her laugh. She didn't do it often enough. 'I promise.'

'I hope that whatever you're promising is something I'm going to approve of,' came a dry comment from the door.

'I didn't hear you knock, Lucas,' remonstrated Scott.

'You must have been having too much fun.'

Scott shrugged, then, seeing Victoria's confusion, decided that the situation only needed a very small prod to make it even more interesting.

'I was going to ask you, Luke—I've decided to get back in touch with a few old friends in Canada and Victoria has said she'll type the letters for me, but she hasn't had much practice and I thought it would probably be easier for her if she used a computer rather than that old manual typewriter of mine. Has the one in your study got a word processing program on it that you could show Tory how to use?'

'Yes, it has...' Lucas said slowly, studying his step-father's guileless expression.

Victoria cringed at his obvious reluctance. It matched her own. 'Oh, but I'd rather mess around with a typewriter than a computer. I've never used one before, and I don't think I'd be very good.'

Lucas turned his thoughtful look on her. 'There has to be a first time for everything,' he pointed out softly.

Victoria's eyes jerked away from his to conceal the sinful thought that suddenly flitted into her mind. How appalled he would be if he knew she was inventing double meanings for his most innocent remarks. It was wicked to even wonder what it would be like for a woman to lose her virginity to a virile, sexy man like Lucas Grey... or to ponder on how and where and with whom he lost his. Somehow she couldn't imagine Lucas as a fumbling virgin. He was probably as intuitive about sex as he was about science...

'I'm considered a rather good teacher...'

Her horrified eyes jumped back to his and for an agonised moment she thought she had spoken the forbidden thoughts out loud. Then she realised he was still innocently talking about the computer.

'Yes, yes, I'm sure you are, but you're very busy with your research. I'd only be taking up your valuable time,' she said feverishly.

She was no match for the combined determination of father and son. As Lucas pointed out with inescapable logic, even conquering just basic computer skills could be very useful to her in the future. And Scott made her feel she would be letting him down if she didn't take up the offer, hinting that if she did, composing his letters wouldn't leave him any spare time over the next few weeks to snoop...

So it was agreed that for an hour every day, while Scott was resting, Victoria would learn how to run the computer and increase her non-existent typing speed with a typing-tutor program.

Luke was as able a teacher as he had promised: patient, detached, good-tempered. It wasn't his fault that Victoria didn't seem to be able to grasp the essentials. It wasn't his fault that her fingers seemed to be all thumbs on the keyboard when he sat beside her or that the software seemed to be as confused by Victoria as she was by it. It wasn't his fault that he was a hideous stumbling block to her progress. *He* seemed to have no problem—working industriously over his incomprehensible equations on the other side of the desk while she plodded laboriously through the exercises set by the fiendish electronic tutor. It didn't seem to bother him that their legs occasionally brushed under the desk or their hands sometimes bumped reaching for the coffee-pot that a suspicious Iris Ransome kept constantly replenished. His powers of concentration were formidable, his mental agility magical and his physical adaptability a model of decorum.

He made her want to scream.

The only time Victoria found she made any worthwhile progress was when Lucas was out. Even though Gabby was, by David's strangely glum account, running the company highly successfully there were still meetings that, as a major shareholder, Lucas had to attend, and it was during one of his absences that Victoria drove herself to new heights of modest achievement creating and nesting her files. When Lucas got back she would casually stun him with her new expertise, she decided as she smugly shut down the computer.

She was humming cheerfully as she arranged some flowers in a vase on the hall table—the one task in the larger house that Iris had actually *volunteered* to relinquish—when Lucas dashed through the front door and into his study. Used by now to the random, explosive eruptions of ideas that rendered Lucas periodically blind and deaf and dumb, Victoria continued serenely composing the full-blown, fragrant blooms. She was admiring the effect against the cream walls of the hall when she gradually became aware of Lucas standing beside her with a very strange expression on his face...

'Didn't your idea work out?' she asked sympathetically. When Jason received a poor exam mark for no reason that he could divine he wore a similar look of pained bafflement.

'Where's Scott?'

'Asleep, I think, why?'

'And have you been arranging flowers all that time?'

'Why, no. You said I could practise on the computer when I had nothing else to do and——'

'Would you come in here for a moment, please?'

Victoria put down the pruning shears and followed him obediently.

'Would you turn on the computer?'

Victoria felt a quiver of unease. She did as he asked and breathed an inward sigh of relief when the crisp monochrome screen glowed to life.

'Could you open the hard disk for me?'

She punched a key and little symbols dotted the screen. Perhaps Lucas had taken a peek at her cleverly stacked files and was teasing her with this mock gravity.

'And now my RX780 file.'

She hesitated, reading the screen. 'There isn't one.'

Lucas folded his arms. 'No, there isn't, is there? And that's very odd, because there was a file called RX780 there when I left this morning. A file that contained all my data and notes and projections for *this*...' He cocked his head at the bank of equipment along the wall. 'A very important file,' he added, in case she hadn't already got the screamingly obvious message.

'*Very* important?' repeated Victoria faintly.

'*Very*. What did you do with it, Victoria?'

'I'm sorry. I must have inadvertently included it with mine. I was transferring files, you see,' she explained hastily, 'with the keyboard rather than the mouse and I must have pulled yours in by mistake. I only did what the manual said. I'll find it right away.' She tapped desperately and they both looked quietly at the small, neat stack of files listed in alphabetical order. There were no Rs.

'It must be in here somewhere. Perhaps I put it in one of your others by mistake.' She hit a wrong key and swore. A very modest swear-word but it shocked them both. Gently Lucas put her away from the keyboard.

'I've already used the Find File command. It's not there. Anywhere.'

'Then where is it?'

'Gone. Vanished. Dumped.'

Victoria's heart plummeted at the ominous words. 'But you have it backed up on floppy disk,' she urged nervously. 'You always told me to back everything up.'

'So I did. And here it is.' He held it up. 'And do you know what?' He inserted the disk into the mouth of the computer and immediately the 'damaged disk' logo appeared.

'That wasn't me. I didn't touch that disk,' Victoria defended herself quickly.

'Didn't you?'

His eyes were black, unblinking, his uneven mouth curved cynically even though his voice was very, very gentle.

Victoria swallowed and shook her head.

'So the fact that I found this disk over *there*——' he pointed to a slim black piece of electronic equipment '—instead of on the desk where I left it has nothing to do with you.'

Victoria opened her mouth to agree, then closed it suddenly.

'Victoria?'

She looked at him miserably. 'I tidied your desk,' she admitted. 'I shifted some things over there while I was doing it.'

'It's not your job to clean this room,' Lucas pointed out.

'I know. But it was very untidy,' she told him. 'All I did was straighten things out a little. I must have forgotten to put the disk back. But I didn't drop it, or anything like that.'

'Do you know what's inside here?' Lucas put his hand on the strange black box, stroking it almost tenderly.

Victoria shook her head. She had the feeling she didn't want to know.

'A magnet. Quite a powerful magnet.'

'Oh.' Even Victoria knew what magnets did to computer programs. It scrambled them. She looked at him wide-eyed as the full magnitude of the disaster suddenly hit her. Why was he so quiet? Why didn't he yell at her and get it over with?

'Oh, Lucas—I'm so sorry. All that work. And it's my fault . . . I don't blame you for feeling awful. Have I wrecked your project? Will you have to start again? I— I can understand if you feel you can't trust a person who carelessly cost you weeks of research... Of course you can have my resignation——'

'No!' He was yelling at last. It was almost a relief.

'But...there's nothing else I can do, Lucas. No way I can make up for what I cost you. I don't know anything about computers—that's what caused this mess. I told you I would be no good at it. I told you I wasn't a very good student and this just proves it. I'll never touch a wretched computer again!' Her voice wobbled alarmingly over the pronouncement. She was blinking so hard she didn't see him reaching out to pull her against his warm chest.

'Don't cry, Victoria, I didn't mean to make you cry, for God's sake.' He groaned as she sniffed valiantly into his shirt-front. 'I can reconstruct the file. I have all the information backed up on other files at Computel; I always take multiple copies as a matter of precaution, it's only a matter of collating it, which won't take very long at all....' His voice was a soothing rumble, his big hand stroking her narrow back. 'It wasn't your fault. I should have locked the thing up with a password as I do at the lab. At the very least I should have filed the back-up in the disk-holder. It happens to us all—losing files occasionally—even certified computer buffs aren't immune. Anyway, it *could* have been a system error...'

Victoria stiffened, and pushed away from him, not quite able to break free but leaning far enough back to see his face. 'You mean it isn't gone forever?'

He shook his head.

'Then why did you frighten me like that by implying it was?' Her former remorse was banished by a healthy wave of anger. 'You can let me go now,' she said haughtily, trying to make up for her ignominious tears.

'I didn't realise you'd take it so badly. I'd forgotten about your martyr complex,' Lucas said drily, aware of his advantage slipping away and determined to keep a firm grasp on the situation, at least physically. How could he tell her he'd intended to indulge in a little subtle emotional blackmail to get her to go out with him, to blatantly manipulate her guilt over a simple mistake to his own advantage? But her swift remorse and stoic acceptance of blame had turned the tables. Victoria, strong and serenely capable in some ways, was appallingly vulnerable in others. Her shy diffidence masked a fragile self-esteem that was very easily undermined by those whose opinions she cared about. And she evidently cared about his. His hopes soared alongside his frustration. He had just managed to get her used to having him constantly around and now, unless he used some very fancy footwork, a rash moment of selfish opportunism was going to destroy all his work. For a soft and gentle creature she had more defences than an armoured tank! He was no longer exactly sure what he wanted from her, but whatever it was he was determined to get it!

'Did your father always teach you to turn the other cheek, rather than fighting for your rights?'

'My father?' The warm hands on her waist were a distraction she could do without.

'The Reverend Mr—what was your maiden name?'

'Bailey—but my father wasn't a Reverend.'

'He was a priest?' Lucas grinned.

'He wasn't a minister at all!' Victoria tried unsuccessfully to ease herself out of his grip but he seemed to have forgotten he was holding her. If she made a fuss he might look more closely and see that her reaction to him was the opposite to what she was trying to project.

'You mean your mother was married twice?' Now it was his turn to be confused.

'No! My father was a historian. My *mother* was a vicar!'

There was a split second's silence and then Lucas began to laugh. The tremors transmitted themselves to Victoria via his stiffened arms, vibrating her in tune to his amusement.

'I fell into a trap of my own despicable male stereotyping there, didn't I?' he said.

'David says that you've always been very determined to employ women at all levels of your company,' said Victoria, responding unwillingly to the confident assurance of his self-derision. Whatever his faults, Lucas wasn't afraid to admit when he was wrong. She mentally added 'flexible' to the list of his accomplishments.

'With Gabby for a sister, how could I do anything else? I think you said you have no brothers or sisters. You must have had a very peaceful childhood...or a lonely one.'

'I wasn't lonely at all.' Victoria automatically defended her parents from the implied criticism. 'My father wrote historical treatises—he worked at home and never minded taking time off to go for long walks, or tell me the most marvellous stories about medieval myths and legends—that was his field, you know. He made history come alive for me in a way that my teachers never did. He was sort of shy with adults but with children he was wonderful—he ran the parish Sunday School. I think he always regretted that my mother couldn't have any more children, but of course the Church helped fill the gap for both of them...'

'So history is your favourite subject?' he said casually, conscious that she had relaxed slightly and stopped fighting his hold. He wanted to draw her closer, but knew that if his body touched hers she would shy away. His only chance to enjoy the warm fragrance of her nearness for a little longer lay in keeping her talking.

'I suppose, but not the dry statistical kind of history you get at school...I like the kind of history you can live, the stories about *people*, the excitement and romance and mystery of the medieval era.' Her voice trailed off dreamily until she recovered herself to add firmly, 'Not that I'd have liked to have actually lived back then...it was far too dangerous and uncomfortable, not to mention downright dirty, even for the nobility.'

'A practical romantic, the best kind to be,' murmured Lucas. 'In marrying a historian I suppose you satisfied both sides of you. What was your husband's speciality?'

Victoria's stomach clenched. She looked away, her mouth unconsciously tightening. 'Modern European history. Would you let me go now, please?'

'Why do you do that?'

'Do what?'

'Get defensive whenever I mention your husband? You never talk about him.'

'I—don't, you're hurting me.' She dug at the fingers splayed around her waist. She couldn't believe that she had let him hold her all this while.

'No, I'm not,' he said quietly. 'I'm trying to understand why you find it so difficult to talk about the past. Were you with him in the car when the accident happened?'

'No.'

'Were you unfaithful to him?'

The question was like a punch in the chest. Her heart pounded alarmingly. 'No!'

He felt the tension drawing her up and away from him and his own tension increased. Was he getting close? He had to know what was behind those defences.

'Was he unfaithful to you? Did he beat you?'

'No! How dare you——?'

'Did he hurt or frighten you sexually?'

How could he be asking her these shameful things? She was shocked and embarrassed. '*No!* Of *course* not!'

'Then why are you so afraid of men?'

'I'm not!'

'You're afraid of me. You won't let me close...'

She froze, icy dread chilling her trembling limbs. 'I work for you.'

He brushed aside the feeble prevarication. 'Why aren't there any other men in your life, apart from your stepsons? I asked David one day whether you dated and he looked at me as if I was a pervert...as if he was *afraid* for you...'

'Oh, God, you didn't...' Victoria's vision blurred in horror as she realised why David had been keeping such close tabs on her working hours lately. He had also continued to insist that her first duty was to him and Jason, with what she had thought was a purely selfish regard for his own creature comforts. Now his brooding concern took on an entirely new dimension.

'I was curious.' It wasn't an apology. 'I can understand Dad going through what he has, at his time of life and in his physical circumstances, but you're young and healthy, you still have most of your life ahead of you. You've been a widow for three years and you haven't been out with another man, except to lunch with me——'

'That wasn't a date!' she said, much too quickly.

'No, but why should the very idea upset you so much? Even if you loved your husband to distraction, surely by now you've come to terms with the fact that he's——'

'Stop it! Please. I don't want to talk to you about this——'

'Why?' There it was again. That insatiable scientific lust not just to speculate, but to *know* all...

'Because it's nothing to do with you.' Her shattered whisper warned him she had had enough and his voice gentled.

'And if I want it to be? I might be able to help...'

If only he could. It was beyond anyone's power to do that. Victoria wasn't aware of the blank despair that turned the rust-green eyes olive drab, she only knew of the forbidden turmoil inside her. He was being kind, she reminded herself. He felt sorry for her. The rest was her wilful imagination. She mustn't let herself weaken now. She owed it to Joshua, to David, to all the family to hold herself together for as long as humanly possible...

'Lucas...' That sounded soft, trembling, feminine...no way to deal with his gentle forcefulness. 'All I want is to be left alone!'

'And do you always get what you want, Victoria?'

She drew a deep breath and felt his fingertips against her lower ribs, his palms cupping her sides, felt his strength and warmth and vibrant life flowing into her, spreading through her cold body, melting her resistance. Lean on me, he seemed to be saying. But she couldn't.

'It's bad for people to get what they want all the time...' she said harshly.

'There speaks the vicar's daughter. Do you know what I want?'

Her imagination running rampant, she shook her head dumbly. He smiled, a sexy quirk of his uneven mouth. He let her go and stepped back and she found that she could breathe again, and think . . . and her first thought was that she felt utterly abandoned.

'I want you and your stepsons—both of them—to come to Scott's birthday dinner. Since you had so much to do with preparing his surprise, it's only fair that you should be here to see us spring it.'

He was inviting her because he knew it would please Scott. The empty hollow in her chest was quickly filled with forced relief. 'I—he knows something is going on, he got that much out of me,' she admitted. 'He promised he wouldn't snoop but I think he suspects——'

'I'm sure he does. But that's all part of the fun, and we've only got until next Wednesday to hang on. When is *your* birthday, by the way?'

She hesitated, then smiled tentatively. 'Christmas Eve.'

He tilted his head. 'It figures. What a lovely gift to wake up to at the end of the bed on Christmas morning.'

Victoria remembered his big, luxurious sunken bed and blushed. 'It was more of an unpleasant shock. Not only was I four weeks premature and very scrawny, but I chose to gatecrash my mother's busiest time of the year!' It had been the family joke, because she had always known that to her parents she was a precious gift from God. Nostalgia led her to confide, 'My birthday treat always used to be going up to the city to see a Christmas pantomime.'

'You like the theatre?' He picked up the lingering note of wistful wonder in her voice.

'I don't go very often. J——' She stopped, then forced herself to go on. 'Joshua used to take me sometimes, but more for my sake than his enjoyment—he often used to fall asleep in his seat! When Maxine and Tracey were home I sometimes went with them . . .'

'Computel is a sponsor for one or two professional theatre groups, so we always get complimentary tickets

for performances. In fact I have a couple here, for
Saturday fortnight: *She Stoops to Conquer*. Would you
like to go?'

Victoria's eyes lit up, but only momentarily. 'You
mean, go with you?' she probed warily.

His thick black lashes masked his flicker of anger as
he responded with barely a pause. 'I thought that you
might be able to use them both—perhaps with a friend—
or one of your stepsons...?'

'Well, David is no more keen than his father, but Jason
might like to go.' Victoria let her excitement at the
prospect bubble over, uncaring that her choice might be
revealing her paucity of friends.

Lucas had found the tickets in the drawer of his desk
and passed them across to her before she could change
her mind.

'These are for the opening night!' Victoria discovered.

'Yes. Is that a problem? All it means is that there's a
supper afterwards during which you can meet the cast.'

'But don't you have to dress up? I don't know if I
have anything suitable,' said Victoria, thinking of her
modest wardrobe.

'It's festive but it's not that formal. These days people
wear whatever they like to an opening; whatever you
choose you won't feel out of place.'

'But... what about you? Don't you want to go?' she
made herself ask. 'Or don't you like going to live
theatre?'

'I love it,' he said warmly, then paused before adding
blandly, 'But I have other plans for that night.'

'Oh.' A woman. The faint sexy French burr that laced
the Canadian drawl told her that as clearly as if he had
said the words. Who was she? One of the glamorous,
sophisticated, clever colleagues that David said Lucas
regularly dated? Lucas admired Gabrielle's ambition and
intellectual achievements, so it stood to reason that he
would expect no less from his own circle of female
friends.

Oh, well, at least that put all her silly fears to rest.
So much so that she found herself not only accepting

the tickets but also dinner on behalf of David and Jason. She was sure they would want to go to Scott's birthday if she said she was going—David to keep an eye on her and Jason to satisfy his curiosity about the man who had created so much dissension in the West household!

CHAPTER SIX

'I DON'T believe I've mentioned how attractive you look this evening, Victoria.'

Victoria smiled uneasily at Lucas as he looked down at her. Flanked by Jason and David on the leather couch, she felt that he couldn't have picked a worse time to deliver his compliment. Still, the amount of alcohol swimming around her system had relaxed her sufficiently to allow an inner surge of heady pleasure at the admiration in his eyes.

'Thank you,' she murmured shyly.

'Dark green suits you,' Lucas went on, holding her softened gaze. 'It's the colour of your eyes when you're feeling...disturbed.' He paused, then added provocatively, 'Like now.'

'She's not disturbed, she's embarrassed,' said David tartly. 'She's not used to fending off trite social flattery.'

'I'm not surprised, if you think that paying a woman a sincere compliment is trite,' said Lucas smoothly, replenishing David's glass from the bottle of champagne he had opened after dinner—the third of the evening. 'When was the last time *you* told Victoria that she looked lovely?'

David scowled as Gabrielle, elegantly sprawled opposite, added with a decided edge, 'Oh, David is a great one for not saying what's on his mind; he thinks that people should have to work that out for themselves, don't you, David? It would never occur to him to actually come out and *say* what he was thinking. Why, that would be too easy...'

'If I said what I was thinking some of the time you wouldn't be flattered at all,' said David curtly.

Victoria sighed. It was going to be an even longer evening than the one she spent here if David and

Gabrielle were going to continue needling each other the way they had all through dinner. Evidently they were on the brink of yet another argument, this one apparently concerned with the number of broken dates caused by Gabrielle's new responsibilities.

'She only bought the dress yesterday, didn't you, Tory?' said Jason, judiciously ignoring the tension. 'I told her she had to have something new to wear to *She Stoops*...'

Victoria went pink as everyone looked at her new dress, thankful that the flimsiness of the fine, silky embossed jersey fabric allowed her to feel cool, even though the sleeves were three-quarter-length and the neckline high. The little stand-up collar was deceptively demure until she moved, revealing the narrow slit from the covered button fastening the collar to her cleavage. The waistline was self-belted, below which the skirt was full to the knee. In colour and cut it was different from her usually restrained style of dress, but she had Gabrielle to thank for that. Gabby had given her the name of the manageress of a boutique where she had an account and Victoria had been putty in the woman's experienced hands, and somewhat taken aback by the reasonable price of the garment she was finally persuaded to buy. If she had been more knowledgeable about designer clothes she would have realised the price was *too* reasonable, but Victoria had innocently accepted the explanation of markdown prices for models that had been used in fashion shows.

'I don't think I thanked you for giving us those tickets, Lucas,' Jason went on. 'I haven't been to a good play for ages.'

'Actually I gave them to Victoria; you were purely incidental,' said Lucas blandly, and Jason grinned. Thank goodness *someone* in the family was at ease among the undercurrents, thought Victoria wryly.

'To Dad, for always being there...even when he shouldn't have been!' The knowing smiles that Lucas and Gabrielle exchanged with Scott over the toast made Victoria even more curious about the circumstances that had welded them into a family. 'May he have many more birthdays, even more surprising than this one.'

'If that gym has anything to do with it, I'll be out-lasting all of you,' Scott joked. He had been shown his present, with due ceremony, before dinner, and even though he had obviously been prepared to feign a certain amount of surprise for the sake of his children Victoria had seen that he was genuinely stunned by the scope and sophistication of his own personal gymnasium. He was especially delighted by the spa pool and sauna, custom-built to cater to his desire to be independent. From now on Scott would be able to have the physiotherapist call on him rather than vice versa.

Scott's voice had shaken with emotion and there had been unashamed tears in his eyes as he thanked Gabby and Lucas. Even David had been touched, temporarily relinquishing his moody formality to shake the elderly hand and warmly wish Scott well.

'I don't see that I can dare be anything else with all this around,' Scott had said, his leathery complexion flushed with unhidden delight. 'Victoria, do I see your hand in this somewhere, aside from putting me in strife with the pool company?' he chuckled.

'It was all Lucas's idea,' said Victoria, bending down to kiss his damp cheek warmly as she laid a soft package in his lap. 'I'm afraid my gift-giving runs to the far more mundane.'

Scott had liked the thick white towelling robe that she had given him to use in his new gym, and Victoria was glad that she hadn't balked at the price tag. It was more than she had ever spent on Joshua, or any of the children, but she had wanted something that expressed to Scott her value of his friendship, her gratitude to him for giving her a chance to cautiously try her wings. Her new con-fidence in herself was rooted in the discovery that she was perfectly capable of surviving outside the protective cocoon the family had spun around her. She could support herself and cope with new responsibilities on top of the old ones without collapsing under the pressure.

More importantly, she was learning to say no and mean it—to David, to Lucas . . . and, more latterly, to herself!

Victoria noticed with surprise that her champagne was gone, and frowned. Had Lucas refilled her glass as he had the others? If so, she didn't recall it. He had perched himself on the arm of the couch next to Jason with the half-empty bottle, so she waggled her empty glass out at him in imperious demand.

'I don't think you should give her any more,' said Jason in a low voice before Lucas could oblige. Victoria was very disappointed in him. He sounded just like David when he spoke in that stuffy tone of voice. She shot him a reproachful look.

'I'm thirsty,' she told Lucas stubbornly, still holding out her glass.

'You're tipsy,' murmured Jason, who had been virtuously drinking water, since he was doing the driving. 'She never drinks at home,' he explained to Lucas. 'I think she feels it would be a bad example to set before a larrikin university student and his friends.'

'Don't be silly,' said Victoria with a primness that sat oddly with her flushed face and sparkling eyes.

'Champagne can give rather a kick to the uninitiated,' said Lucas, selfishly withholding the bottle.

'I am perfectly initiated,' she told him with a crispness slightly blurred by the difficult consonants. 'I have had champagne before, you know.'

'When?' He seemed to doubt her word.

'When I got married,' she said triumphantly.

'One glass,' Jason added annoyingly. 'It was the first time you'd ever had alcohol and it put you out like a light.'

'That must have made for an exciting start to the honeymoon,' said Lucas drily, and Jason told him blithely,

'Oh, they didn't have a honeymoon. Dad had to dash off on a lecture tour the day after they got married. He promised you'd go away together some other time but you never did get around to it, did you, Tory? There was always Stevie, or one of us having some sort of crisis to prevent you.'

'We didn't need a honeymoon,' said Victoria stoutly. Except for David, old enough to understand the situation without being told, none of the West children had known the true reason for their father's hasty marriage. Although the girls had been periodically upset by malicious comments at school they had been too young to appreciate the damaging implications of the local gossip that had blown up about the widowed professor and his young 'housekeeper'. When Jason had started getting into fights on Victoria's behalf and they had had a visit from a concerned social worker, Joshua had decided to take protective action. What he had proposed had been couched in the most gentle and unthreatening terms that he could manage, but gossip had only been the catalyst, not the true reason for Victoria's acceptance. Innocent as she was in experience, in perception she was mature beyond her years, and knew that although there was no romantic love in their relationship there was a deep respect and friendship that transcended the difference in their ages, and which could grow into something safer and more enduring than passion ... something like the tender love her parents had shared. With all the children at home she had never lacked in hugs and appreciation. In spite of the twin beds in the master bedroom their marriage had been rock-solid, and that secure foundation had enabled Victoria to grow from girl to woman in her own slow time. When Steven had died and Joshua had cried in her arms Victoria had sensed the vital shift in the balance of their relationship. The time was right to assert herself as an equal partner. She had gone out and bought a double bed and shyly seduced her own husband. It had been as tender and fulfilling as ever she had hoped and Joshua had admitted that he had been waiting for her to make the first move towards a deeper intimacy between them. He had been a gentle, kind lover, touchingly uncertain of his ability to satisfy his much younger wife. Victoria had reassured him generously, looking forward to creating a life that would cement the new bond between them. Instead...

'Victoria?'

Lucas was staring at her with a strangely tight face and Victoria realised that she had drifted off in the middle of a conversation. She hurriedly tried to remember what she had been going to say but was rescued from her embarrassment in a most dramatic way. There was a crash and a sharp screech from the hallway.

Slightly impeded by champagne, Victoria was almost last on the scene and was immediately sobered by the sight of Iris Ransome lying amid a wreckage of coffee-cups and the hand-made chocolates with which she had planned to top the superb meal that she had worked all day to prepare. Fortunately the silver coffee-pot had fallen well away from her body, the hot liquid steaming into the carpet at the bottom of the stairs.

Lucas was firing off orders. Stiff-lipped, Iris admitted that the minor pains in her abdomen that she had been stoically enduring for a week had suddenly become excruciating.

While David phoned for an ambulance, Gabrielle fetched a rug and Lucas knelt and held Iris's hand, calming her tearful apologies, saying exactly the right things to soothe her shattered dignity.

'I'm sorry...all this mess,' panted Iris as they all milled anxiously around her. 'If that coffee isn't cleaned up——'

'Don't you worry, Iris, we'll look after everything,' interrupted Gabrielle, tucking the rug around her solid limbs.

'You don't know one end of a mop from the other,' the injured woman gritted doggedly.

Lucas, whose hand she was clenching in her powerful grip, didn't even wince. 'No, but Victoria does. She'll help out, won't you, Victoria?'

'Of course I will,' she said readily.

'We can manage——'

'Huh!' In the circumstances the snort which cut off Lucas's easy reassurance was a Herculean effort at nor-

mality. 'Remember what happened last time I went on
holiday? The house was a wreck and Mr Scott had
stuffed himself with all sorts of nonsense and had a re-
lapse. None of you even knows where I keep the vacuum
cleaner!'

'I do,' said Victoria, then flushed as Lucas looked
sharply at her over his shoulder. The faint wail of a siren
sounded in the distance as his eyes narrowed. His sudden
smile was dangerously bright.

'Victoria can look after us. You wouldn't mind doing
that for Iris, would you, Victoria? Moving in for a few
days so that she doesn't have to worry about us as well
as herself.'

'You mean *live* here? As your housekeeper?' David
spluttered. A part-time job was one thing, but Victoria
as a full-time domestic was too much to take! 'That's
impossible!'

'I'd pay you the going rate, of course,' said Lucas,
ignoring him, not taking his eyes off Victoria's startled
confusion. Surely he didn't think that her misgivings had
anything to do with mere money?

'No! I mean, I'd be happy to help. . .' she stammered.

'Of course she would, but she doesn't have to live in,'
said David hastily, suddenly conscious of how callous
his knee-jerk reaction had sounded.

'No, but it would be far more convenient, not to
mention easier for Victoria.'

'But—what about us?'

'Er—David——' began Jason nervously, seeing the
battle looming.

'What about you?' Gabrielle demanded, her brown
eyes flashing. 'Aren't you capable of managing for
yourself for a few days? What do you expect Victoria
to do—go home after a demanding day's full-time work
here and cook *your* dinner and do *your* laundry?'

Her shot was so accurate that David went brick-red.
Victoria felt sorry for him. It wasn't that he couldn't do
those things—only that he had never needed to. 'It might
be more than a few days,' he said defensively. 'And it
doesn't sound as if you ever do your own cooking or

laundry, either, so there's no need to sound so self-righteous! Why don't *you* pull your weight at home for a change?'

'I happen to be running quite a large corporation, quite competently in fact, although it seems to have escaped your notice,' Gabrielle pointed out icily. 'I don't have time to play housewife. Not every woman is cut out to be a perfect little homemaker, you know.' It was obviously a sore point between them. 'I never realised you were so selfish. I suppose next you're going to suggest that *Dad* starts "pulling his weight" with the house work——'

David valiantly ignored that slur. 'I happen to be thinking of Victoria's good name. What are people going to say about her living here with two men...?'

To everyone else the remark obviously sounded ridiculously old-fashioned, but Victoria's heart went out to him as she realised the source of his misguided anxiety.

'David, it's not like——'

'You really are like something out of the Dark Ages!' Gabrielle snapped. '*I* live here, too, but I suppose I don't count as a woman because I don't wear an apron.'

'I don't know what the problem is with you two,' Lucas rapped out as David began to bluster, 'but this is not the time or place to air it. Not only are you upsetting Iris but you're being damned insulting towards Victoria. She does her job every bit as well as you do yours and deserves respect for it. She is also quite capable of speaking and acting on her own behalf. So what either of you think or believe is her place is irrelevant. It's entirely up to Victoria. Victoria?'

She felt a strange warmth at his unexpected defence of her, but it was the fear and pain in Iris's eyes she responded to rather than Lucas's subtle challenge.

'I hope you don't mind if I come and see you as soon as you're settled in hospital, Iris,' she said with deliberate wryness. 'You'll have to let me know all your routines and timetables so everything isn't turned around when you come back. I might not meet your standards, but I should be able to keep things on an even keel if I know you've still got one hand on the wheel, even if it's by remote control . . .'

The ambulancemen had arrived and there wasn't time for Iris to reply, but Lucas paused on the steps before he climbed into the ambulance and took Victoria's hand.

'That was very kind of you, Victoria, but then I expect no less of you,' he said quietly. 'You put her mind wonderfully at ease. Sometimes she gets anxious about getting old—not that I'd ever use that as grounds for asking her to leave; she's practically one of the family—but it makes her hide what she thinks is any weakness by acting tough and ultra-possessive. Thank you for understanding . . .'

Oh, she understood all right, and one of the reasons she did was now arguing with Gabrielle, who wanted him to follow the ambulance to the hospital.

'I just don't like hospitals,' David was saying aggressively.

'My God, you're not much use in a crisis, are you? All you can think about is yourself! Would it make any difference if it was *me* being rushed to hospital?' Gabrielle cried in disgust. 'I don't suppose I'd ever see you again!'

David went white. 'I'll drive you there but I won't come in,' he said tightly.

'Don't bother!'

In the end he did take her, in the red Jaguar, leaving Jason to take Victoria home in David's car so that she could pack a few belongings for her temporary stay. On the way Jason tried to reassure her of any doubts raised by David by reminding her that he had once been a boy scout, as if that made him an instant housekeeping expert. Victoria had an idea that Jason's fond memories of camping out hardly coincided with her own notions of good diet and hygiene!

When she arrived back, she found that Scott had already chosen her a very pleasantly furnished room, next door to Gabrielle's.

'And thus we observe the proprieties,' said Scott with a twinkle, tilting his head towards Lucas's door down the hall. 'Even your stepson must be satisfied.'

'David isn't really as reactionary as he sounds.' Victoria felt bound to offer an explanation. 'It's just that—well, he's had first-hand experience of how little justice there is in careless gossip, how dangerous and destructive it can be. It's made him——'

'Protective of you. Yes, we can all see that.' Thankfully Scott didn't probe for the reason, although Victoria had the feeling that he *did* see, all too much. 'I know that I'm the reason you agreed to stay,' he teased lightly. 'If it were just Luke and Gabby, I suspect you would have rather enjoyed telling them that it would do them both good to fend for themselves...' He laughed as Victoria pinkened at the truth of his statement.

'Actually I think that David and Jason are in more need of the lesson,' she admitted. 'I hadn't realised how much I had been spoiling them since the girls moved out. I don't suppose their future wives would thank me for not expecting them to do their fair share around the house...'

It was, as David had predicted, going to be more than 'a few days' before Iris Ransome came home. The nagging pain that she had been swallowing indigestion tablets for was a rumbling appendix which had finally ruptured. After her operation Iris was quite ill for some days, and when she realised that she faced an enforced convalescence she gave Victoria a long list of detailed instructions and settled down to stoically suffer the food and service at the private hospital to which Lucas had had her transferred. There was a telephone at her bedside and she didn't hesitate to ring Victoria to find out if things were being done the right way, the *only* way. Victoria didn't mind. She suspected that Iris, who had belligerently refused to take a real holiday for years, was beginning to enjoy the unaccustomed rest free of worry about 'her' family, the more so when Iris's widowed cousin from Wellington travelled up to stay with her son.

Usually, now, when Victoria popped in to visit it was to find the two old women knitting and gossiping furiously about the son's abortive attempts to find a wife, the terrible inefficiencies of the nursing staff and the wretched state of a modern world where people didn't know what real hard work was!

That certainly didn't apply to Victoria. Her own pride made her determined not to give Iris cause for complaint when she returned, even if it meant spreading herself a little thinly for a while. Scott was marvellous, making as few demands on her as possible, brushing aside her insistence that she was being paid for all her extra work by helping out where possible. He even decided that it was time he stopped putting himself at the mercy of other people's schedules and began taking driving lessons in a car equipped with specially adapted hand controls.

Although Victoria had decided to accept the offer of an increased wage for her temporary duties so that everything was kept on a strictly businesslike basis, her employers had continued to show a regrettable ignorance of the proper behaviour. Gabby, whipping in and out of the house in a whirlwind of energy, treated Victoria more like a long-suffering friend than an employee and Lucas was just . . . Lucas, a law unto himself. He had reacted badly when Victoria had at first insisted on eating in the kitchen, as Iris had always done.

'People don't eat with their housekeepers,' Victoria had said flatly, when Lucas strode through to the kitchen the night after she had moved in, demanding to know why she wasn't sitting down to dinner with them.

'Don't be such a snob, Victoria,' he had glinted angrily. 'Servility doesn't suit you.'

'But a servant is what I am,' she said stiffly. 'You're paying me to do a certain job, the *whole* job, not just the parts of it that suit my convenience.'

For a moment it looked as if he was going to snatch her off the kitchen chair and march her into the dining-room. She lifted her chin and stared at him bravely. She had accepted his offer of an increased wage with this very situation in mind.

He had turned on his heel and walked out without argument, leaving her staring at her suddenly unappetising meal. She had won the first small confrontation so why did she suddenly feel like the loser?

Five minutes later she knew that it was because she *had* lost. Luke was sitting opposite her with Gabrielle and Scott on either side, the elegant dinnerware looking ridiculously out of place crowded on to the small kitchen tabletop. Victoria was as mortified as Lucas had meant her to be and thereafter she had meekly taken her meals with the family. Even at breakfast Lucas insisted on her sitting down properly for her coffee and toast, instead of rushing to and from the kitchen.

It was becoming increasingly difficult to pretend that Lucas was just the man she worked for. She was very careful not to infringe his privacy. She never left her room unless she was fully groomed and preferably armoured in her apron, but Lucas had no such scruples. He came to breakfast in the mornings in a black silk robe and matching pyjama bottoms, when Victoria knew very well from the laundry load that he didn't wear pyjamas. Or he came in from the pool, or a session in Scott's spa, with a towel wrapped low around his lean hips, his thickly muscled torso gleaming like oiled silk, the tight black curls on his chest glistening with droplets of moisture. The hair was just as thick on his forearms and legs and his thighs looked hard and powerful. Victoria had never seen so much hair on a man—David and Jason had both inherited their father's hairless chest—and she found it almost impossible to respond naturally if Lucas paused for a casual word at such times. He seemed so very much at ease with his body, perhaps he didn't realise how overwhelmingly obvious his masculinity was, how threatening...

But a worse self-betrayal was to come. On the opening night of *She Stoops To Conquer*, Victoria was ready early because Jason had announced with great ceremony that he was going to take her out to dinner first. When she had discovered that, in her absence, David and Jason had been existing on TV dinners and takeaways, Victoria

had weakened and sent over several heat-and-eat cas-
seroles. Gabrielle had told her flatly that she was mad
to pander to their shameless male manipulation of her
sympathies but Victoria was amused to note that Gabby
wasn't above a bit of pandering herself. That very night
she was intending to cook a meal for David and Scott,
although the very basic nature of the cookbook and the
stark simplicity of the menu she had shown Victoria
showed that she had no intention of letting it become a
habit!

Victoria was sure it wouldn't have occurred to Jason
to offer her culinary proof of his gratitude if it wasn't
for the fact that Lucas had pointedly asked him on his
last visit to his stepmother where he was taking her for
dinner on such a special occasion. He had even rec-
ommended a good restaurant which he assured Jason
wouldn't break the bank. Although annoyed by the interference, Victoria hadn't protested. She had never
grudged the time or effort spent on her family, but it
was nice to be actively appreciated for a change!

After she had put on the new green dress Gabrielle
had appeared in a suspiciously spattered apron, and
frowned at the shining free-fall of her hair.

'Oh, no, you can't go like *that*. It has to go *up*!' she
had said, and proceeded to do it with deceptive simplicity, using one of her own glittering clips to secure
the knot on top of Victoria's head and then teasing
strands out around her forehead and ears and the nape
of her neck to soften the look. Then she had produced
some emerald and diamond earrings from her apron
pocket, clipped them on to Victoria's tender lobes, and
sailed back to the kitchen, deaf to all objections. Victoria
had hardly recognised the elegant lady in the mirror and
couldn't help feeling rather excited as she left her room
to go downstairs and wait for Jason.

As she passed the door to Lucas's bedroom she heard
the soft sound of classical music playing on his radio
and hesitated. He was going out tonight too, where and
with whom he hadn't said, and Victoria, anxious to
maintain a respectful distance between them, hadn't

asked. Unfortunately nor had Scott or Gabby, usually casually inquisitive about each other's comings and goings, asked him in her presence. Common courtesy dictated that she thank him again for the tickets before she left she told herself, as she impulsively knocked on his door. It was not because she wanted him to see her in all her finery!

But the door wasn't quite closed and her first light blow caused it to swing open, revealing an empty bedroom. The radio mounted over the sunken bed played softly and the dimmer switch had been adjusted so that the recessed overhead spotlights were reduced to a mellow glow. Even just standing in the doorway Victoria received such a strong impression of romantic intimacy that she almost recoiled. Perhaps Lucas was planning an evening in tonight, with his sophisticated lady of the moment!

At that moment Lucas stepped out of his bathroom and a hot tide of sensation washed through Victoria's body. He had obviously just come out of the shower and he was nude. He was lithe and tanned, his freshly towelled skin faintly glossy under the soft spotlights. There was nothing draped around his hips, this time, to disguise the flagrant maleness and Victoria looked. She couldn't help it. The hair on his chest narrowed to a thin line bisecting his taut belly and then flared dramatically out again, a dark, thick, soft cradle for his masculinity. It was a startling contrast to his inner thigh where, with every step, a patch of skin the size of her small palm flashed pale and bare...vulnerable, enticing to her eyes. The tiny glimpse of softness was eclipsed as he began to turn towards his wardrobe and she saw the smooth flex of his hip, the pale ripple of his hard, muscled buttocks, the twin dimples at the base of the long, flexible spine.

Victoria should have turned and fled, but she was rooted to the spot by the sight of such brazen magnificence. Her breathing became quick and shallow and a flush spread across her cheeks. How long she stood there helplessly staring she didn't know but it must only have been a few seconds before Lucas sensed something and turned his head. She knew that he had seen her, because the beautiful body that fascinated her stilled, every muscle tensing. A panicky heartbeat later he was walking towards her across the room, taking his time, making no attempt at modesty.

Victoria's legs had no strength and her oxygen supply was running dangerously low. She felt a prickling inside her skull and knew that if she tried to move she would probably swoon at his feet! The blood rushed and roared in her ears. She couldn't tear her eyes away from him as he approached, without haste, like a predator confidentially stalking a mesmerised prey, and as he came towards her his body changed in a way that finally shocked her out of her trance. Her eyes jerked to his face and she saw it there too, the hungry stirring of male arousal, the sudden voluptuous fullness of his crooked mouth, the sexual knowledge in the hot dark eyes that stripped away all her pretences and plunged to the heart of her deepest desires.

He knew. He was going to respond to her secret need. Touch her. Reach out and pull her into his arms, his room...shut out the world with his mouth. She already burned with his heat, she could already feel the hairy roughness of his naked flesh, smell the unique, musky scent of their mingled pleasure...

So it came as a drenching shock when, still holding her tremulous gaze, Lucas gently closed the door in her face.

Victoria listened to the snick of the lock in drowning disbelief. It freed her locked limbs and she began to shake. She pressed a fist to her mouth to stop herself moaning out loud in agonised embarrassment, slumping against the wall. God, she had been caught drooling over him like a sex-starved teenager, invading his privacy, inviting his scorn and derision. No wonder he had locked the door on her. Why, she was little better than a peeping Tom!

Victoria went hot and cold with shame, torturing herself with the knowledge that she had probably lost all his respect. Ogling him hadn't been enough, oh, no she had to issue a tacit sexual invitation with her refusal to apologise or leave—albeit because she had found herself without voice or power of movement! He had been mildly stirred by her wide-eyed gaze, but the calculated deliberation of that closed door reaffirmed all she had learned of him. He was a man, not an animal, a highly discriminating and intimidatingly intelligent individual. He would require mental as well as physical stimulation from his lovers. He didn't take a woman just because she indicated she was available. And that was how she had acted. Available. His for the taking. But it had been a momentary aberration. She wasn't anybody's for the taking... and especially not his!

Terrified he would come out and discover her wallowing in her humiliation, Victoria rushed along to the bathroom and quickly splashed her hot face in cool water. She reapplied the light covering of make-up, cringing as she confronted the lingering sensual awareness in her eyes. She was a perfectly normal woman; she had speculated about men before in a sexual way, but never so vividly and never about someone real. Always before it had been some safe, hazy, fantasy figure in her dreams, a man who was completely under her control, and who never made her feel awkward or unwanted or shamefully wanton!

By the time Jason arrived to collect her the hot flushes had mercifully vanished, but shame still sat like a rock in the pit of her stomach.

Fortunately Jason didn't seem to notice that he was escorting a scarlet woman out to dinner. He ate the gratifyingly large servings with relish and teased Victoria about how well he and David were managing without her.

Their theatre tickets were for the stalls and after insisting that they get there well in time for the performance Victoria had to read her programme several times over as they waited for the seats around them to fill up. Until almost the last minute she thought the two seats next to her were going to remain empty, but suddenly Jason was galvanised in his seat.

'Hey, look who's here! Why didn't he tell us he was coming too? Hello, Lucas! Are you going to be sitting with us?'

CHAPTER SEVEN

LUCAS had dressed up—black dinner-jacket and tie—but as he eased himself along the crowded row all a horrified Victoria could see was acres of bare, hard flesh, crisp dark curls, and burgeoning arousal. Two spots of bright colour burned on her cheekbones as she forced herself to meet Lucas's unreadable eyes, trying to hide the desperation in hers by lifting her chin defiantly.

'Good evening, Victoria,' he said pleasantly, as if he had forgotten that she had made a humiliating exhibition of herself only two hours before.

'I thought you said you had other plans for tonight,' she accused stiffly, forcing herself to speak just to prove that she wasn't utterly devastated by his unexpected appearance.

'I do. And here she is. Tanya, this is Victoria West and her stepson Jason. Tanya Jacobson.'

A woman peeped around Lucas's broad shoulder, all eyes and blonde curls and flirtatious mischief. Victoria's confidence shrivelled further under her falsely elegant façade. She hadn't even noticed the woman that Lucas had in tow. No, not a woman, a girl, thought Victoria with a small shock as Lucas sat down beside her and Tanya remained standing for a few seconds longer, so that everyone in the vicinity might get a thorough appreciation of her sleek figure in a strapless black cocktail dress. She couldn't be over eighteen, Victoria thought with a small spurt of acid as she watched the young girl innocently preen. Lucas was practically cradle-robbing!

'Isn't this great?' Tanya grinned at Victoria as she flounced down on the other side of Lucas in a rustle of taffeta and leaned familiarly across him to talk. Victoria could see out of the corner of her eye that one of the girl's exquisitely manicured hands was resting on Lucas's hard thigh. 'I love opening nights. I love plays full-stop. Did you see the last one they did here?'

Victoria shook her head, speechless with a fresh surge of shame. No wonder Lucas had rejected her, when he had all that eager, untarnished exuberance waiting for him. Tanya wouldn't have any hang-ups, or responsibilities, or old-fashioned notions cluttering up her psyche. She would be free, frank and modern. Victoria was none of those things, despite her recent attempts to prove otherwise, and she suddenly felt old and jaded. Her soft mouth drooped unknowingly.

Lucas shifted in his seat and his thigh briefly brushed Victoria's. She jumped and dropped her programme. As she bent to pick it up Lucas also bent and they battled briefly over it as Jason responded to Tanya's bubbly question above their heads.

'Thank you,' a flustered Victoria snapped as she finally retrieved it from his grasp, and they both sat up again. He was wearing a clean, sharp aftershave but beneath it was the hint of primitive, musky male that she had scented earlier on his naked skin. She opened the programme and desperately began to read the cast-list for the fourth time.

'My pleasure,' murmured Lucas. 'Do you mind if I share?' He leaned closer to get a better view.

'Couldn't you afford one of your own?' she asked, conscious of his brawny shoulder wedged against hers. She was having trouble breathing again.

'I gave it to Tanya.'

The tender amusement with which he said the girl's name gave Victoria a sharp prod. 'Well, share hers, then,' she told him tightly, still refusing her look at him.

'There's no need to be embarrassed, Victoria,' he horrified her by saying very softly into her ear. 'I was the one in the nude, not you.'

'I'm not embarrassed,' she hissed out of the corner of her mouth, hoping Jason wasn't listening.

'Neither am I,' he said in a contented murmur. 'I'm not ashamed of my body. I enjoyed having you look at me with wide-eyed wonder.'

He *enjoyed*...? How *dared* he say that to her after slamming the door in her face? And he was enjoying this mockery just as much, making her so furious that her embarrassment melted into fury. 'That wasn't wonder, that was disgust!' she sneered in a vitriolic little whisper. 'As far as I'm concerned you can take your perverted little pleasures and——'

'Now, Victoria, remember you're a vicar's daughter,' he chuckled softly. 'Lies and profanity aren't in your genes. You know, if you blush any harder your freckles are going to explode——'

The dimming of the lights forestalled any further exchange of conversation and Victoria was left helplessly seething, somewhat appalled at her lack of control. She should have been dignified and ignored the devil's tempting. Instead she had compounded her earlier folly.

In spite of her acute discomfort Victoria soon found herself lost in the comic complications of Goldsmith's plot, ironically aware that the confusion of misunderstandings and deceptions had certain parallels in her own life. It was good to be able to sit back and laugh, and know that it would all work out well in the end. She was so enchanted with the action that she was disappointed when the interval arrived, and she had to bump back to earth.

The theatre itself, though large, with a high, ornate domed ceiling, was old, and the air-conditioning was obviously not quite equal to the task presented to it by a full house. When Lucas suggested they all go to the bar for a cool refreshment before the next act even Victoria was happy to agree. As Lucas fetched their drinks they discovered that Tanya was also at Auckland University, studying architecture, and soon she and Jason were chatting away like old friends about their similar interests. The bar was crowded and somehow Victoria and Lucas were squeezed a short distance away from the two absorbed students.

'She's very attractive, isn't she?' said Lucas, following her gaze.

'Rather young for you, I would have thought,' Victoria was unable to prevent herself commenting.

'You think so?' Lucas contemplated the idea.

At the risk of sounding jealous Victoria said smugly, 'She seems to be more interested in Jason than she does in you.'

'Yes, she does, doesn't she?' He sounded surprised. 'In fact, she and Jason look rather well together, don't they—young, blond, similar interests, both at varsity...'

An awful suspicion was nibbling at the edge of Victoria's consciousness. Lucas seemed remarkably affable for a man who was watching his girl being wafted from under his nose. And not once had Tanya looked around to check up on the whereabouts of her date.

Victoria sipped her drink and looked at him out of the corner of her eye. He was watching her in amusement and she jerked her eyes frontwards again and took another hurried sip. Surely he couldn't have...? No. Surely he was just baiting her again.

'What do you think?' he murmured. 'Should we stand aside and let the young ones enjoy themselves?'

'I happen to be young, too,' Victoria said evasively, her suspicion now taking large chunks out of her meagre self-possession.

'Mmm, but you wear such a sedate air of maturity that I always think of you as ageless.' She didn't quite know whether that was supposed to be a compliment or not. 'Ah, there are the chimes. Shall we go back?' He raised his voice. 'Children?'

The other two grinned and again, by some grand design of the crowd, Victoria found herself hemmed in with Lucas rather than Jason and, when she came to sit down, she found that a mutual rearrangement had occurred so that Tanya was now on the other side of her, next to Jason.

Victoria sat down in her new seat with the utmost of reluctance, her ridiculous suspicion now confirmed beyond doubt. 'Who is she?' she asked flatly.

'The daughter of a man who works for me,' Lucas replied meekly. 'Actually I'm her godfather.'

Victoria simmered, her eyes as green as the emeralds at her ears as she demanded, 'You planned this, didn't you?'

Lucas gave her a crooked smile of triumph as the lights dimmed once more.

'He stoops to conquer?' His smoky amusement drifted around her burning ears as he took her small, slender hand and laced his fingers through his and held it, all through the rest of the play.

Even then there was no escape, for Jason and his new-found friend wanted to enjoy the supper and dancing on the stage that was to follow the show. Victoria was in a cleft stick. She knew that if she suddenly said she wanted to go home she would sound like a kill-joy. Jason would be chastened but dutiful and Lucas was quite likely to come up with the marvellously practical idea that *he* take her home, so that the other two didn't have to curtail their evening. Jason was her stepson, not her date. He didn't have to observe the unwritten social courtesy of escorting home the woman he came with and he would be quite right in resenting it if she insisted.

'Champagne?' Lucas was being solicitous. He had already plied her with delectable savouries from the buffet set up in the theatre foyer, which she had eaten just for something to do with her nervous hands. Her stomach was now doing most peculiar somersaults. Lucas held up the glass and Victoria was tempted to pour it over his impossible head, an impulse which shocked her since she was a very non-violent person.

'I'd rather have coffee,' she told him, sternly resisting the temptation.

'Oh, yes, you don't have much of a head for it, do you? Remember what happened last time you drank champagne?'

'What?' said Victoria, in the most bored tone she could manage.

'You ended up moving in with me.'

A dignified matron in front of them turned and stared curiously at Victoria as she blushed. To her mortification it turned out to be someone Lucas knew and he introduced her without mentioning that she was his housekeeper.

'Who's the snob now?' she muttered sourly as they moved away. 'Afraid to be seen out with the help?'

'I'd like nothing more.' He took up the challenge deftly as he manoeuvred her to the edge of the crowd. 'Would you come out to dinner with me tomorrow night?'

Victoria was stunned. 'I—no—you know I can't——'

'I know nothing of the kind. All I know is that I have to resort to the most ridiculous subterfuges to get you to spend any time alone with me. You made it very clear when I gave you those theatre tickets that if I was including myself in the invitation you wouldn't accept. So I removed your dilemma, and aren't you glad I did? Now, whatever happens, it'll be my fault, not yours...'

That was such a dangerous line of thought that Victoria chose to pursue a petty issue instead. 'We're not alone.'

He shrugged. 'Beggars can't be choosers. How long are you going to continue this farce?'

'Farce? I thought *She Stoops* was a Restoration comedy.' She was no good with banter, especially when the banteree refused to co-operate.

'And I thought maybe you were afraid of sex.'

'*Lucas!*'

'Until tonight. Tonight you looked at me with hungry eyes, Victoria. You wanted me.'

She edged back against a plaster pillar, looking nervously around. They were sheltered here, from the noisy throng, but their privacy was merely an illusion. 'Don't say those things, not here——'

'Then where? In the car? At home? In my room?' His voice dropped an octave and he propped one arm against the pillar, his fingers splayed next to her head. 'In my bed?'

'Lucas, please——'

'I have tried to please you. But every step I take forward you take two back, and if I step back you just stay where you are. What kind of courtship dance is that?'

'Courtship?' Victoria felt a fresh riot in her stomach as she echoed the word in horror. She moved restlessly and his other hand darted up, so that now both arms were braced against the pillar, trapping her.

His smile was this time merely a twitch. 'A figure of speech,' he soothed. 'As I said, I liked having you look at me, Victoria. But you could see that. I wanted to show you just how much I liked having your eyes on me, but I wasn't going to let your curiosity seduce me——' he calmly overrode her infuriated gasp '—into doing something we'd both regret in the morning. I promised myself I wouldn't rush you, and if I had touched you tonight I would have been greedy. I would have ravished you all the way to heaven and back, and to hell with any second thoughts on your part. You didn't want to be ravished. You were all dressed up and looking forward to going out. You came to me to be admired and flattered, not grabbed and devoured. And you don't trust me yet. I'm not going to make love to you until you trust me, no matter how many times you beg me with those lonely eyes.'

Victoria felt more trapped than ever. 'I only wanted to thank you for the tickets, that's why I came to your room——'

'No, it's not.' He refused to accept her self-denial. 'You could have thanked me any time. You wanted me to see you, to flaunt yourself a little. You wanted me even a little jealous that I was going out with someone else and wanted me to see what I was missing——'

'Don't be ridiculous!' She blushed helplessly. Was she really that transparent? Then how was it that she was becoming such a mystery to herself?

'Am I being? I hope not.' His elbows unlocked so that he could lean closer, not touching her with any part of himself yet enveloping her with his warmth. 'I don't know if you're ready to hear this now, but I'm going to tell you anyway: I'm jealous, too. I don't like to think of you being curious about other men, only me. You turn me on, lady, with your sweetly elusive ways and your gentle eyes and your spicy ginger skin. I want you but I don't want to hurt you. I want to know you inside out—how you think, how you feel, why you respond to me the way you do. I don't want there to be any regrets, Victoria, and that's why I don't want anything to be hasty or rushed between us. From the first I knew that with you I wanted it to be long and slow and lasting...'

Victoria trembled at the terrible enchantment his words wove around her aching heart. No man had ever said such beautiful things to her. *He* shouldn't say such things, for to say the words aloud gave them reality and form, the power to move her in new and frightening ways.

'From the first?' Victoria said feverishly, trying not to wonder exactly what he meant by 'it'? Their *affair*?

'The first time I met you. The night I patched and painted you.' His eyes watched his words sink in and continued with increasing roughness, 'I can never use my bathroom now without thinking of you in there, all bare legs and freckles, rumpled and sexy in your embarrassment. You poked your tongue out like a child when you tried to paint your nails, but it didn't make you childish at all. I wanted to bend down and bite it, and then suck it into my mouth. I think about making love to you in my bath, in my shower—hell, anywhere we can fit! I'm spending so much time daydreaming about you in there that I'm the cleanest I've been in years. It's been driving me crazy trying to pretend I don't feel the way I do, so that I don't frighten you off...'

'You mean, all along...?' Victoria was struggling with the implications of his brazen confession. All the time she had been battling against her sinful imagination, convinced that the poor man would be embarrassed if he'd known what was going through her mind, *he* had been deliberately trying to arouse her awareness of him as a man...

'You *meant* to make me think those awful things!' she realised, pressing her hands to her flushed cheeks.

'What awful things?' he asked, his curiosity tempered
by deep satisfaction as he invited huskily, 'What awful
things do I make you think about, Victoria? Things
about you . . . and me . . . ?'

'No! Oh, God——!' To know that she had been indulging in forbidden sexual fantasy was one thing, but
to have it suddenly presented to her as even remotely
possible was shattering. Her stomach churned violently.
'I don't feel—I think I should go. Jason——'

Her white face, her glittering eyes warned him that he
had pushed her to the limit of her endurance and he felt
a surge of the now-familiar rage of frustration. What
was it about him that the thought of intimacy with him
made her shake and look faint?

'All right, I'll find Jason,' he said grimly, making no
attempt to remove his arms. 'But before I do, answer
me one question?'

'Yes?'

'Are you a virgin?'

If possible she went even paler. She looked at him as
if he was quite mad, which wasn't far off, but she didn't
tell him to go to hell. 'No—I told you, Joshua and I
were trying for another child.'

'But only after Steven died?'

'What makes you say that?' she said defensively.

'Just something that Scott mentioned you had said.
And a few things Jason has let slip, and it would explain
David's excessively protective attitude. Was there some
ugly gossip about you and Joshua, after his wife died?'

She lifted her chin in the familiar gesture of gentle
defiance.

'Some.'

Anger thickened his voice. 'More than some,' he
guessed. 'Ignorance can make people cruel. Was it just
talk?'

'There were some letters,' admitted Victoria wearily,
shielding her hurt by lowering her thick lashes, but that
left her staring at his tapering chest. 'And the children
came in for some teasing. Jason was in the seventh form
and he was . . . well, he didn't know how to handle it and

nearly got expelled for fighting—and then the social welfare people got involved...'

Lucas expelled a quiet breath. One veil less to obstruct him from his purpose. 'So you got married.'

'Yes.' She lifted her eyes proudly. 'But I wanted to. I was proud to be Joshua's wife. I never regretted it. Not for a moment.'

'No.' He didn't betray her trust, however unwillingly coerced from her lips. He moved his arm, but only so that his hand could cup her tender jaw. 'I'm sure you were a fine and loyal wife.'

'It might not have been a real marriage from the beginning but it was later; Joshua knew I was ready to accept his love,' she insisted.

'And the child? Was that to replace the one he lost?'

He made it sound like some sort of sacrifice and she shook her head to dislodge his hand. 'No! Steven was——' She showed him her pure, fragile profile as she briefly looked away, her voice struggling. 'Steven was special.'

He leaned against the column beside her, folding his arms across his chest to show her that she was free to move away, free to reject his interest.

'Tell me about him? Was he badly affected? I know that sometimes spina bifida children can lead almost normal lives.' He didn't tell her that he had read several books on the subject when he had discovered about the West child, seeking to find something of Victoria in the experiences of strangers. He clenched his jaw to hide his elation when she didn't take the opportunity to pull back into her shell.

'He almost died when he was born,' said Victoria huskily, helplessly drawn by that soft, almost tender curiosity. 'He had hydrocephalus—that's a fluid build-up in the brain—and quite a severe exposure of the spine. They operated successfully but they couldn't reverse the *effects* of the malformation. Steven was paralysed from mid-chest down and he had speech and motor control difficulties with his hands. He was never very strong and was especially prone to kidney problems, but he wasn't mentally handicapped. He was very bright, always, even when he was very ill. He learned to read and loved listening to music. Miranda wasn't physically strong enough herself to do much with him but she was determined that he would be the best he could be. For that she said he would have to be a fighter, and he was…right up to the end. When he was gone there was a big gap in my life, in all our lives, because looking after him, keeping him challenged and happy took up a lot of time and energy.

'I suppose wanting a child of my own *was* because we had just lost Steven,' she admitted painfully, 'because I needed to fill that gap. We'd always known his chances of surviving into adulthood weren't so good because of his general physical frailty, but there was just no time to think of having other children. Then, when he was gone and the others were grown up enough not to need constant supervision and…well, Joshua knew how much I loved children…'

'Did *he* want to start another family, at his time of life?'

She looked back at him and her eyes were dark and steady, astonished at how much she had opened to him after he had behaved the way he had, threatened the very foundations of her life… 'He wanted what I wanted. He wanted me to be happy.'

'I'm sorry.' He touched her mouth tenderly with his finger, his voice deep and sincere. 'I'm sorry that he died before you had the child of your heart. I'll go and find Jason.'

As he walked away Victoria sagged back against the pillar, anguish streaking through her soul. A child of her heart. How well, and how simply, that explained her need. If she had had a child she might not now feel this terrible loneliness, this growing conflict within herself, the restlessness that made her long for what she should not.

As she had predicted, it was Lucas who drove her home, but she was too weary and relaxed to raise any objections. Somehow she felt her burden had lessened and yet, in another sense, it had increased. She must talk to David. She wouldn't ask, she would tell him how it was going to be from now on. She could no longer trust herself to continue to keep Lucas at bay except with the bitter truth. Her strength had been in his assumed indifference. The knowledge that he wanted her, however fleetingly, was too dangerous for her possessing.

At first they drove in silence but as the lights of the city flashed past Lucas began to talk, and suddenly she was hearing some of his own bitter truths—his confusing childhood—his mother—and the cold, shadowy figure of his natural father...

'She was like a totally different person when my father wasn't around—she laughed, she was warm and loving— but it would shut off like a switch whenever Lennox deigned to notice her. Even as a very young child I knew that she was frightened of him.'

'You mean, he beat her?' That would explain all Scott's biting anger at the man.

'Not physically, no—her parents would never have stood for that kind of abuse. But as long as appearances were satisfied they didn't interfere. No, he was more subtle, he was a clever businessman, a master manipulator, a charming, cold, conscienceless bastard, in fact. He married my mother out of greed and ambition and made sure that she knew it. He undermined all her confidence in herself, denied her any life of her own and then taunted her with being boring and insipid, a failure as a person and as a wife. Never in public, of course. In public he was the perfect husband with his nervous, neurotic wife.' He smiled mirthlessly. 'I suppose he didn't consider Gabby and me important, because we were allowed to witness his emotional cruelties. Perhaps he expected us to despise her as much as he did; instead we despised him, even though we didn't fully understand what he was trying to do.

'I suppose I must have been about twelve when she first met Scott. Considering what Lennox had put her through, and her own strong principles about marriage, it wasn't surprising that she asked him for a divorce, but he wouldn't hear of it. Nor would her parents. They were afraid of the scandal. It was far less of a scandal for people to think that their daughter had mental problems. Lennox cut off her allowance and credit and hinted around that she was unstable, that she had gambling and drinking problems. He threatened her with committal if she opposed him and convinced her that she'd never be able to win a custody fight. So for our sake she hung on. Endured.' His voice echoed with a strong pride. 'But she refused to stop loving Scott, or to give up hope they could be together one day. I don't know if they were lovers or just friends for all those bitter years under Lennox's thumb, and I never asked. It was enough to know that if ever I had a problem or wanted advice I could always trust my mother's friend Scott for an honest answer. My so-called father believed children should be seen and not heard. That's why Gabby and I called Scott Dad from the day he married Mum—because he had already earned the title. I was an obnoxious rebellious teenager as far as Lennox and my grandparents were concerned, and when I came of age and they realised that if it came to any mud-slinging I would happily provide buckets-full they lost their hold over Mum. Besides, by then Lennox had spent Mum's fortune making his own. She walked out of that marriage with nothing, even though it meant cutting herself off from her family and starting a new life in a new country——'

'But you work for the family company—are your grandparents dead?'

'My grandfather is.' His dim, hard profile showed regret but no deep sorrow. 'After I got my doctorate and had worked in computers for a few years he wrote to me, offering me management of Computel. Mum was an only child, you see—no other heirs, except for some second cousins.' His wry smile acknowledged the expediences enforced by harsh reality. 'I didn't want anything to do with them, but Mum was never capable of bearing a grudge. Even Lennox I think she pitied more than hated—it was what kept her sane all those years

against all his efforts to prove otherwise. Also she felt
guilty that her actions had denied Gabby and me our
rightful inheritance. So I went... And I found two tired,
lonely old people who had found that money and social
position was no substitute for flesh and blood. I stayed
in Canada for a while learning the ins and outs of
Computel, but one of the second cousins is a genuine
financial whizz-kid who'd worked his way up through
Computel from scratch. I felt very strongly that an accident of birth shouldn't deprive him of the position he'd
earned. So I agreed to accept the New Zealand Division,
although now with rationalisation we actually work very
closely with Head Office in Montreal...'

Victoria was still trying to picture this powerful man
as a bewildered child—a rebellious teenager—struggling
to cope with raging hormones and the turbulent emotions
of a boy who despised his own father. But he had had
Scott as a strong, honourable paternal image, and
Victoria had no doubt that, even within the uncertain
morality of their situation, Scott had been a man of
honour... like his son. Victoria looked out into the
darkness of the night, her eyes blurring with tears.

'Victoria?'

They were home. She hadn't even noticed him turn
into the drive. She fumbled for the door-handle and
scrambled out of the white BMW, feeling horribly vulnerable at the knowledge that he was no longer just the
cardboard cut-out of a man that she had insisted on
seeing him as, for the sake of her own peace of mind.

Instead of driving the car around to the garage, Lucas
got out too, catching up with her just as she made the
shadowy sanctuary of the front porch. She fumbled for
her key in her small bag.

'Victoria——?'

He didn't have to tell her what he wanted; it was
written all over his hard, handsome face.

'No, Lucas——'

'Just a chaste kiss, on the doorstep...'

Chaste? How could he say that when every time he
simply brushed against her she felt a tumult of feeling
that was as far from chaste as it was possible to be?

'I can't. You don't understand——'

'Not yet. But I'm trying, little mother, I'm trying...'

He put his mouth to hers and it was as chaste as he
had promised, a light stroking of her sealed lips that was
warm and sweet. She trembled at the sweetness. He
placed a hand in the small of her back to steady her,
and used the other to lightly cup her breast, and she
gasped and he plunged swiftly into the undefended ter-
ritory, filling her with the hot taste of his tongue, fuelling
and feeding on the heady rush of sensation that exploded within her. His hand began to move on her breast
as his mouth moved on hers, firmly, slowly, erotically,
with a languorous rhythm that made her moan softly in
her throat. The soft pads of his fingertips found her
tautening nipple and rubbed it lovingly through the
slippery fabric so that little needles of pleasure injected
her with drugging passion. She shifted in his arms, but
only so that she could lift her own hands to his shoulders,
reaching out for the forbidden fruit that she had glimpsed
that afternoon with an abandoned eagerness that would
have shocked her if she had been capable of conscious
thought. The kiss deepened abruptly to a kind of consummation, a woman accepting the savage thrust of a
man inside her body. The gentle eroticism with which
Lucas had begun the assault was swiftly overtaken by a
primitive need to stake his claim, to stamp her with the
image of his sexuality. His thighs were hard against hers,
the hand on her back sliding lower, moving her hips
forward to acknowledge his blatant sex. At the same time
Victoria could feel his heart pounding like a jack-
hammer against the solid wall of his chest and her fingers
curled against the fine tremors that shivered across the
thick muscles of his back and shoulders, not in resistance, but in an equally primitive exultation in her feminine power.

He moved, pressing her back against the wall of the
porch, holding her there with his body as he wrenched

his mouth away and said roughly, 'You see what I mean? I have trouble controlling myself...I wondered how you'd taste. Now I know.'

He was breathing hard, his rigid body trembling almost as violently as hers. His chest rose and fell under the black jacket as he fought for control. Slowly he began to draw away, but at the last minute he couldn't let her go completely and as his hand slid away from her breast he inserted a wistful finger into the slit at her cleavage, stroking down the soft slope to the barrier of her lacy bra and up again. She was swollen and tender and had to clench her teeth against the feverish desire to beg him to ease the ache properly.

'So rich and ripe and creamy soft,' he growled thickly. 'One taste isn't enough. I want more. Much more.'

'Lucas——'

His finger brushed her hard nipple and was gone. 'It's too late to fight it, Victoria,' he said with gentle finality. 'I'm not the only one left wanting more. You have the taste for me now, too. Don't starve us both. I have to go to Wellington first thing tomorrow, for some damned seminar,' he murmured regretfully. 'But when I come back, darling, we'll feast on fulfilment...'

Victoria spent a tormented night. Lucas was a ruthlessly brilliant strategist. He had battered down her defences and then, instead of taking her by storm, had forced her to confront her own vulnerable emotions. He wanted an equal partner in passion. But to Victoria fulfilment meant love, and she wasn't in love with Lucas. She *couldn't* be. And she couldn't let herself think that the 'more' he spoke about might be an emotional commitment she wasn't free to give.

The next morning she was unutterably glad that she hadn't given in to her tumultuous emotions. The doctor's voice was chillingly emphatic on the other end of the line.

'I think you should come down as soon as possible, Mrs West, preferably immediately. I need you to make some very important decisions about your husband. We can't delay any longer...'

Joshua. Her heart quivered under the blow. Joshua needed her more than Lucas ever could. He was her husband, her honour and her duty. While he lived, nothing in the world must be allowed to tempt her to betray him!

CHAPTER EIGHT

VICTORIA had learned not to hate hospitals.

Once she had seen the ugly, functional concrete buildings and the clinical efficiency of the staff as cold and depersonalising and had deeply resented the medical profession's arrogant assumption that only someone with a medical degree could properly understand the process of treatment.

Now, after three years of almost daily contact, she knew differently. Sometimes the brusqueness of the staff was due to fatigue but most often it was simply a defence mechanism. Compassion was a prerequisite for the job, but too much of it was a definite handicap in a place where the death of one person meant that an empty bed was to be filled again, probably immediately, and someone else nurtured through their pain and fear. Victoria could even understand the doctors who, in the early days after Joshua's accident, had refused to speculate on his chances. At the time the waiting and not knowing had caused her terrible anguish, but now she was grateful to the doctor for not holding out false hope, or frightening her with a bleak prediction of the future. If she had known then that these three years would be a day-by-day vigil over an unconscious man, that there might be a lifetime of waiting, of not knowing, ahead of her, her strength might have failed.

In those first few weeks before Joshua's condition had stabilised she had existed in a state of abnormal calm, dazed by shock and disbelief. She had not been ready to assume any further burden of knowledge. Instead it had come to her gradually, so that, by the time she fully accepted that 'no discernible brain activity' meant a coma that neither she, nor the doctors, had any control over, she was ready to move to the next stage, quietly ad-

justing to the strange state of being a wife, yet not a
wife, shouldering the responsibility of helping Joshua's
children re-weave their own lives around the tragedy. She
had succeeded with them all except David.

David, who had been at the wheel of the car the night
his father was plunged into his indefinite night. David,
who had had a couple of drinks beforehand—not enough
to put him over the legal blood-alcohol limit but enough
to sicken him with guilt, even though the police had said
that an accident was unavoidable on his part—a van had
blown a tyre and swerved head-on into the car. David's
reactions had been quick enough to take evasive action,
but the van had clipped the front passenger side of the
car, which had flipped down a bank into a muddy stream.
Miraculously David had suffered only mild concussion,
but Joshua had not been so lucky. For a while they had
thought he would die, and as far as David was concerned Joshua *had* died that night... killed by his own
son. Even now he could not bear to face his perceived
sin by visiting the silent, unresponsive shell of a once-
vibrant father.

In the beginning a grief-stricken Jason, Maxine and
Tracey had visited daily with Victoria to read aloud, and
play tapes or just talk to their father in the hope of triggering his return to consciousness. But after months of
no progress, during which several attempts to take Joshua
off his ventilator had failed, their natural youthful spirits
had begun to strain against the enforced extension of
semi-mourning. On the advice of a hospital psychol-
ogist, Victoria had gently encouraged them to pare down
their visits and resume more normal lives. They had been
able to do so, secure in the knowledge that Victoria would
continue to be the torch-bearer of their hope. Each
afternoon she spent a few hours at Joshua's bedside, her
loyalty as strong as her stepchildren's faith in her. In
return they lavished her with their sometimes overwhelmingly protective support, and if a tiny part of her
recognised more than a tinge of collective guilt in their
attitude she was glad to provide a harmless outlet for it.

When the girls had hesitated about their trip to Australia Victoria had reminded them that Joshua—and Miranda—had always wanted their children to be strong and independent as well as loving and loyal. Joshua would not have expected them to put their whole lives on hold for his sake, she pointed out, and they could still send tapes that she could play him, and letters she could read to him during her regular late-afternoon visit. That he might not have wanted his young wife, either, to forfeit any hope of a future happiness for herself never even entered her head. Victoria took her vows to love and to cherish very seriously.

Now, sitting in the doctor's office, she had to face the hardest decision of her life. She didn't want to make it, but she could no longer ignore it.

The bright torch that she had loyally taken up had finally dimmed. Some patients in a coma survived for decades in their state of suspended animation, but for several months now Joshua had been deteriorating in small but telling ways. In spite of the carefully balanced nourishment his body received and the passive exercises that the physiotherapist had taught Victoria to put the slack limbs through each day, Joshua had been gradually losing condition. As she had shaved him and washed him, and helped the nurses dress him and turn him in the bed to prevent pressure sores forming Victoria had noticed the wasting, but when the doctor had first approached her she had refused to countenance his suggestions.

'There's just no more time left, Victoria,' the doctor reiterated quietly. 'Joshua's condition has reached the point of no return. From now on, organ degeneration will be irreversible, and you know what that means...'

'You're asking me to let my husband die!' She had fought for so long for Joshua to live that it was second nature to resist. Her valiant spirit had forbidden her even to contemplate that his death might be a kind release... for both of them.

Dr Martin's face was set in familiar lines of tiredness. They had had this discussion a number of times before and each respected and understood the other's position, but now it was no longer a discussion of mere principle.

'But not in pain and not in vain,' he said gently. 'You've already signed the donation forms. In a few hours they may become worthless because there's no point in transplanting even slightly impaired organs into people already weakened by their illness or disease.'

'"May"; you said "may",' said Victoria, knowing from the compassionate expression in Dr Martin's eyes that she was clutching at straws. The forms she had signed soon after Joshua's accident had been a step in this direction, but then she hadn't been aware of the looming abyss. 'That means there's a chance it might not happen. There's a chance he might——'

'Hang on for years? It would be a miracle, Victoria. I know you have a strong faith, and I know that medical "miracles" happen every day somewhere in the world, but he's slipped too far away from us.' He took her hand, and held it, hard, offering her his sympathy, his powerful conviction. 'We fought the good fight, Victoria, and we lost. But at least we can snatch some sort of victory from the jaws of defeat. Joshua can be someone else's miracle... a number of miracles, in fact.'

Victoria's eyes were blurred with tears and she struggled to hold them at bay. She couldn't be weak now. She had to be stronger than ever!

'What about the rest of the family, Victoria?' Dr Martin said gently. 'I know you've discussed this with them on a general basis. I don't want to take unfair advantage of your vulnerability right now—apart from anything else it would be unethical—but I *need* a decision. We can't store a liver the way we can kidneys. It has to be transplanted within hours.' He hesitated, then went on softly, inexorably, 'We have a tissue-typing match with a woman in the transplant unit right now. If she doesn't get a new liver within a few days she's going to die. She's in her twenties. She contracted the hepatitis C virus through a blood transfusion and it destroyed her own liver. She has a husband and a fine year-old baby daughter. She wants to live so much, Victoria, and she can...if we give her this most precious chance.

'This is a time for families, Victoria. Call for yours. You don't *have* to make this decision alone...'

'David would never even discuss it,' said Victoria painfully. 'And how can I ask Jason or the girls to make that sort of decision, knowing how David feels?'

It was David's fixed perception of his original guilt that led him to actively lead people to assume that both his parents were dead, thus rejecting their lacerating pity and imagined accusation. Victoria had accepted his attitude only because she had been unable to change it, and because his self-deception had never directly affected her before. That he had not told the woman he said he wished to marry that his father was still alive had come as a disturbing shock. Only too late had Victoria realised what an uncomfortable charade her habitual deference to his 'problem', and her reticence about her family in that initial interview with Scott, had committed her to. The fact that inevitably Gabrielle—and Lucas—would learn the truth was a thought that Victoria had deliberately blinded herself to. *Lucas*... Even just thinking his name was dangerous to her ragged self-control...

'And yet you expect it of yourself...' Dr Martin said with the abruptness of one who knew her well. 'Give them credit for three years' more maturity, Victoria. You don't have to protect them any more. They're all independent adults, and I think you'll find that sharing this burden with them will ease it for all of you...'

His pocket beeped and he had to rush away. He left Victoria drinking sweet, hot tea with the day sister on Joshua's ward, a middle-aged woman she had become quite friendly with over the years, albeit at a mutually respectful distance. Seeing Victoria as pale and rigid and artificially calm as she had been three years before, Sister 'Who Knows' Best took the matter into her own capable hands and before she knew it Victoria was being enfolded in Jason's warm embrace. She didn't even have the strength to berate Sister Best for her presumption.

Jason was accompanied by the vicar who had married her and Joshua and who had been a kind presence in their lives over the years. Victoria had been quietly active in the local parish, even when Steven was demanding much of her attention, and now she was glad that she had never faltered in her faith. The Reverend Michael Avon was supremely at ease with his calling, always receptive, never judgemental or condemning. He was aware of their family situation and deeply conscious of her moral dilemma. She knew that, whatever her decision, he would stand by her.

'I'm sorry...David wouldn't come.' Jason hugged her tightly, his voice thick and muffled. 'He said he didn't have any right to be here...bloody blind idiot! I rang the girls. They're trying to get a flight back as soon as they can...but they send their love. They know we'll do the right thing. Oh, *Tory*!'

She hadn't seen Jason cry for a long time and it was like a jagged rock shattering her glassy self-possession.

'I don't know what to do!' she cried, the tears pouring down her face at last. Her mother, her father, Miranda, Steven...the litany of loss chanted through her mind. And now Joshua. Now they wanted her not just to let him go, as she had had to let the others go, but to perform a positive act of release. She might tell herself that whether he lived or died after they turned off the ventilator was God's will, but could she believe it?

Jason didn't let her go, needing the closeness as much as she did, and Victoria realised that Dr Martin and Sister Best had been right. Denying herself family support had been selfish, as well as needlessly self-sacrificing. What Lucas had brutally called her 'martyr complex' at work!

'I don't even know what *is* right and wrong any more!' she whispered brokenly.

'Dad would know,' said Jason roughly. 'He always seemed to be able to look problems clear through to the other side.'

His gruff words sparked in her mind, illuminating a new avenue of thought.

Perhaps the decision wasn't theirs to make at all, but Joshua's. All the agony she was going through was on her own behalf, on behalf of those who would be left behind to grieve. She was trying to make a decision based on what was best for *them*, she realised with a stabbing shock, not what was best for Joshua. To Joshua, mere existence had never been enough. Man was created to explore, to create, to grow and change with the seasons. Intellect *was* man; without it he was nothing. That was Joshua's firm belief, reaffirmed by his study of history. Did he not have the right to die by the principles he had so fiercely lived by? More than once he had privately told Victoria that he envied little Steven his immense courage, that he himself would loathe any restriction on his intellectual or physical freedom. He had hated being even the slightest bit ill. The idea of total suspension of mind and body and soul would have been horrifying. Freed of the prison of his stricken body, might not his soul be able to soar again? And if in doing so his body could provide new life for someone else would not Joshua's generous spirit rejoice? Victoria thought of a bereft husband of a mortally ill young woman. She thought of a motherless baby girl taking her first faltering steps into an uncertain world. Her heart hollowed in her chest, but for the first time suffocating fear and uncertainty didn't rush in to smother rational thought.

Maxine and Tracey arrived, exhausted by their frantic trip across the Tasman, late that night, but by then Joshua West had slipped away as quietly as he lived for the past three years. He survived for only minutes after the ventilator was disconnected and there was no battle to hold his tentative grip on life, no sign of distress or change in his peaceful expression. It took some moments for Victoria, tightly holding the smooth, pale hand, to realise that the end had come, and she let Jason quietly lead her away, conscious that something within herself had died at that moment too, some small flickering ember of hope that had kept smouldering despite all the odds.

She felt frozen, aware of everything going on around her but strangely unable to relate to it. She felt nothing. Her lack of emotion disturbed her, especially around Maxine and Tracey who, although they admitted having been long prepared for their father's death, were still able to mourn naturally and openly. Jason, too, cried without apology, and even David was able to finally express some of the shame and anger that he had locked away. Victoria felt separated from them, shut out, as if Joshua's death had wiped out the years of belonging. Surely if she really and truly *belonged* in the family she wouldn't feel this disconnected emptiness? She felt almost resentful of their easy display of grief, when it was she who had borne the brunt of their father's illness, she who had provided him with the daily love and care that enabled them to forget.

To hide her shocking lack of feeling and inappropriate anger, Victoria insisted on carrying on as usual. She had rung Scott before she left the hospital, and embellishing on the vague excuse of the illness of a friend with which she had explained her hasty departure that morning, was reassured that Gabrielle was there and that of course she must put her friend first. But her first night as a widow under the family roof only increased Victoria's sense of alienation. She didn't sleep at all, her mind in a cold turmoil of unresolved panic. In the morning she was conscious of the odd looks she was getting as she cooked everyone an unwanted breakfast and shrank from the thought of the ugliness their loving probing might reveal. She didn't notice the warning look that Jason sent around the startled table when she said briskly that since the girls were here she could go back to her job with an easy mind.

'The Greys are relying on me and it's probably best that I keep myself busy,' she said, scraping the uneaten food away.

Even David heeded his younger brother's silent command. 'I'll handle the arrangements, Victoria,' he said quietly. 'Dr Martin said it would be a few days

before . . . I . . . we won't be able to have the funeral until
at least Wednesday.'

Three days. Victoria explored her all-encompassing
numbness. Surely she would find some tears by then, if
only for appearance's sake? Surely she would feel something other than this dreadful, icy relief that it was all
over?

As it was she thought she coped rather well. The most
difficult hurdle was Lucas, back from Wellington and
concerned to hear from his stepfather of her absence the
day before.

'Was it one of the children?' he asked, waylaying her
outside his study almost as soon as she walked in the
door. 'I would have called last night to ask, Victoria,
but I didn't get back until almost midnight.'

'Children?' she faltered. She always thought of the
four Wests collectively as 'the children', but she didn't
think that Lucas did, and his personal concern took her
by surprise. Out of sheer self-defence she had blanked
the other night out of her mind. Lucas had never been
anything to her, or she to him, but employer and
employee.

'At the hospital,' he clarified carefully. He had noted
the shadows under her weary eyes, the vulnerable
tightness of her mouth, the stiff set of her shoulders,
but knew he could do nothing unless she opened up to
him.

'What hospital?' she said numbly. Did he know? Had
David told Gabby? She searched his face and saw nothing
but compassionate enquiry, and . . . was that . . . *guilt*? Her
heart chilled even further, contracting from the source
of her pain.

'The one you visit every day. You go there to spend
time with handicapped children, don't you? I saw you
there, playing with them. Was it one of them?'

'You saw me there?' she repeated tonelessly, her cold
lack of reaction sounding like a grim demand.

'All right, so I followed you one day last week,' he
admitted roughly. 'I wanted to know why you insisted

on a few hours off every afternoon and why you refused
to say where you were going.'

'You spied on me?' she whispered, shocked by the
revelation. It was true she usually called in at the long-
stay children's ward whenever she had visited Joshua,
but it was just as often after as before. If Lucas had
followed her to Joshua's ward . . .

'Yes, dammit! And don't bother to tell me I should
be ashamed of myself because I'm not,' he exploded.
'I'd do it again if I had to. I *will* do it again if it's the
only way I can penetrate that reserve of yours. Why
didn't you tell me? Was it because you didn't want to
talk about Steven? Well, you've told me all about him
now, so that's one obstacle out of the way. I think you're
brave and incredibly generous to give of yourself the way
you do.'

'No—I——' The words stuck in her guilty throat.

'I thought it might have been some man,' he said, his
dark eyes swerving away from hers in self-disgust, his
voice deep and gritty. 'In spite of what I knew about
your integrity I thought you might have been seeing
someone . . . a lover.'

She began to laugh, a high-pitched sound of despair,
and he looked back at her sharply.

'I'm sorry for thinking that. But I'm not sorry for
discovering the truth——'

Victoria had cut him off, unable to bear the mockery
of being praised for her integrity. He knew nothing of
the truth and when he learned of it he would be as disgusted by her behaviour as she was. That she had told
herself it was for David's sake was no excuse. She had
let Lucas kiss and touch her as if she was an unmarried
woman. She had been unfaithful in thought, if not in
deed with him. She had almost turned them both into
adulterers by her deception. No amount of rationalising
could excuse the fact that while her husband was dying
she was falling in love with another man and contem-
plating becoming his lover! And, at some deep level of
the subconscious, that lover had been with her when she
had made the fatal decision to let Joshua die!

That knowledge polished the impervious surface of her reserve. It gave her the strength to ignore Lucas's attempts to thrust deeper into her consciousness, to turn all his demands and enquiries away with a soft, indifferent answer. She was living strictly for the present, moment by moment, miraculously able to walk and talk and work as if she was a real person, not just a hollow dummy going through the motions. She knew that Scott and Gabby were puzzled by her suddenly distant courtesy, but they were so kind that she suspected that Lucas must have mentioned his theory about one of the children at the hospital and felt more of a fraud and impostor than ever.

The day of the funeral was bright and clear, the first real hint of autumn sharpening the air. Michael Avon led the small private service movingly, and when David got up to give the eulogy Victoria was dreadfully afraid that he would not be equal to the task he had doggedly set himself.

Her hands twisted in her lap as he began awkwardly to speak, but soon they stilled. David spoke of his father with love and affection, as an honoured memory, unadulterated by the conflicts that had raged within himself during Joshua's long incarceration. It was a hymn as much of praise as of sorrow, and when he came back and took his place beside her again Victoria took his trembling hand and pressed it gratefully. He smiled at her, and in doing so looked so much like Joshua that at last the welcome flood of cleansing emotion swept over her. As they stood at the graveside she was able to shed her bitterness and subconscious sense of anger in slow, hot tears that were her tribute and final farewell to the man who had once been Joshua West.

David had behaved so impeccably during the service that it came as a shock when, back at the house with the small number of mourners who had been invited to partake of a modest wake, he helped himself to several stiff drinks in swift succession. He had never touched hard spirits since the night of the accident. Now it seemed he was making up for lost time.

'He'll be OK, Tory,' whispered Maxine, looking wan but relaxed under the gloss of her newly acquired Sydney sophistication. 'He's just letting off steam. It's about time, don't you think?'

'It doesn't seem to be doing him much good,' said Victoria, nodding vaguely as she farewelled some almost forgotten colleague of Joshua's. With every drink David looked moodier and more withdrawn.

'Here, you look as if you could do with one yourself,' said Jason, putting a glass into her hand. 'How are you feeling? You look as if you're about to keel over?'

'I'm holding up.' She smiled at him automatically.

By the time the last guest had left she felt light-headed with exhaustion and with the rising tension in the front room where David sat steadily drinking.

'Don't you think you've had enough?' she finally murmured.

'Why? I'm not driving anywhere.' He laughed grimly, slumped in the easy chair that had always been Joshua's favourite.

'You'd better not, either, Tory,' said Jason. 'That whisky I gave you was a double. I'll take you back when you're ready to go, OK?'

David jerked up in the seat. 'Back where?'

'I told Scott I'd be back tonight,' said Victoria tentatively. She had considered asking for several days off but Maxine and Jason had convinced her otherwise. They had both noticed the way she had clung to her job as a lifeline and decided that for once Victoria was acting purely on instinct. She was seeking solace where she most wanted to find it. When Jason murmured something about home being where the heart was to his sisters they were immediately intrigued by the possibilities.

'Scott...or Luke?' sneered David, and Victoria went pale.

'Hey, David, take it easy,' said Tracey, looking from one to the other uncertainly. She adored her big brother but she, like Maxine, realised that Victoria had as much right to break away from the sorrows of the past as they had. More, in fact...

'You've been away, you don' know,' he said heavily. 'Tory's s'posed to be working for Scott but she spends more time with Lucas, don' you, Tory? He doesn' know she's married, see——'

'That wasn't her idea, David——'

Jason's hasty intervention only served to twist the knife. 'That doesn' mean she has to carry on like that. I seen the way he looks at you, and you look right back, don't you, Tory?' he slurred with a sudden surge of raggedly focused rage. 'You want him. Tha's why you're so keen on skivvying for him, 'cos while you're with him you c'n forget about the rest of us . . . about Dad . . .'

Victoria was too weary and saddened by the knowledge he hadn't yet conquered his demons to be shocked by his increasingly wild and incoherent ravings with their bitter element of truth. She would have tried to reason with him, but the others quietly rallied round their stepmother and removed her to the kitchen where they fed her another restorative whisky while they decided what best to do. Victoria sat in the passive grip of a kind of exhausted serenity as they agreed that, sober, David was stubborn enough; drunk, he was totally intractable. They decided to let him work through his drunken rage before they bluntly told him what they thought of his taking out his self-pity on Victoria. Maxine offered to take her to the Greys' while Tracey cleared up the mess and Jason babysat his brother.

'There's no sense in you staying on anyway, when he's like this,' said Jason as he hugged her by the door. 'I'll sober him up and he'll be grovelling by morning, you'll see. He thinks the world of you, Tory . . . always has . . . he's just hurting. It's finally hit him that Dad's gone and that he wasn't there at the end because of his own stupid determination to punish himself for something he didn't do!'

Maxine wasn't entirely happy leaving her at the Greys' gate, but Victoria wearily reassured her that all she wanted to do was fall straight into bed.

'Maybe I can meet the Greys another time,' said Maxine. 'From what Jason's said this Gabby seems to be tying David up in knots. Poor Dave, I never thought he'd dance to the tune of a career woman; he's always shied away from forceful, argumentative females.'

Her screaming omission made Victoria smile wryly in the darkness. It was probably Luke that Maxine was most intrigued about. The idea of another man 'looking at' Victoria hadn't seemed to shock her at all. Victoria felt a fresh wave of love for her stepdaughter break over her.

'I don't think the dancing is all on his part. Gabby is pretty mixed-up, too, but in spite of all their battles they keep doggedly trying to figure out how to handle each other. I guess if Gabby can survive learning that he lied to her about Joshua they might have a genuine chance together. At least it will help her understand why he sometimes feels unworthy of her love and pushes her away and then turns around and acts like a macho idiot afraid to let her out of his sight...'

Maxine didn't drive away until she had seen Victoria go inside. The house was quiet and Victoria realised it must be later than she had thought. She looked at the watch on her slim wrist and saw with a shock that it was after eight. She couldn't remember whether she had told Scott that she would be home to cook dinner. In fact, she found she couldn't really remember anything that had happened over the past few days. Her mind had gone blessedly blank. She leaned back against the door, quietly conscious that a great weight had been lifted from her shoulders, leaving her weak and light-headed. She tried to summon the strength to move forward, to face the inevitable...

'You're back.'

The quiet voice issued from the door to the dining-room. The inevitable, it seemed, had been lying in wait for her. Lucas. She didn't know if she could fend off his curiosity tonight.

'Yes.' She didn't offer any explanation of where she had been, and to her weary surprise he didn't ask. He moved out from the dimness of the room behind him into the light of the hallway and she got another surprise to see he was wearing a tea-towel tucked into the top of

his dark trousers. In spite of the coolness of the evening
he wore a thin, loose white shirt that shimmered slightly
in the light.

'You look tired.'

'I am. I was wondering if anyone would mind if I
went straight to bed...I'm sorry about dinner...I just
don't feel up to——'

'Gabby took Dad out. They've gone to a show and
then she's dragging him off somewhere trendy for
supper.'

'Oh.' She pushed away from the door and frowned at
the slightly weaving floor. She didn't realise that it was
she who was weaving, her fragile air accentuated by the
plain black dress, her eyes glittering in her flushed face.

Lucas stepped closer, but he didn't reach out to
support her. Tonight he intended to knock every support
out from under her. He could see that she was exhausted
but that only hardened his resolve. Whatever had happened today, wherever she had been, she could keep her
secrets. Tonight he wasn't going to ask questions that
she could refuse to answer. Tonight he wasn't going to
let her drift quietly past him with a serene, empty smile
as if he was a stranger she couldn't quite place. Tonight
he wasn't going to let her shut him out the way she had
for the past few days. His trip to Wellington had been
unavoidable but it had lost him all the ground he had
struggled so hard to gain. In his absence all her defences
had slammed back into place. His ego had taken a vicious
battering over this woman and enough, he had decided
grimly, was enough. Her wistful air of shy vulnerability
wasn't a defence, it was a weapon with which she was
slashing him to pieces. But he had an equally superior
weapon. Sex. She could play hide and seek with his
gentlemanly honour indefinitely, but if he discarded it
she would have nowhere to run. He had been trying to
get her to trust him enough to conquer her inhibitions.
Now he knew the error of his ways. Her inhibitions only
lasted as long as his restraint. When he kissed her she
melted like wax in his arms. She had wanted him so
fiercely the other night that she had shaken with it. If

he had taken her then she would have *had* to trust him. Where words had failed, action would prevail. If it took a cold-blooded seduction to lure her into trusting him then...so be it. He felt the ruthless excitement grip him as he looked down at her, knowing what he was going to do.

'Well...' Victoria took an unsteady step, made uneasy by his continued silence.

'You've been drinking,' he realised, identifying the faint aroma of whisky with a surge of possessive fury that he swiftly quelled. It didn't matter where she'd been or with whom. She was here now...for the taking. 'Have you eaten?'

'Eaten?'

'Food.' He deliberately gentled his voice. She evidently hadn't. Drink on an empty stomach. A sitting duck. Still, he didn't want her to blame the alcohol for what she was about to do. 'How long since you had a proper meal? Did you have lunch?'

'No...I...goodness, I don't know...' Victoria was grateful that there was a sound reason for the floating euphoria that underpinned her exhaustion. 'No wonder I feel so odd.'

'I suggest you have something now, or you're going to feel even worse later on.'

'I really only want to go to bed...'

So do I. 'After you've eaten,' he said firmly. 'I've been slaving over a hot stove all evening; the least you can do is taste my efforts.'

'*You* have?' Victoria let him steer her towards the dining-room. 'I didn't know you could cook.'

'You never asked,' he said quietly.

He sounded almost hurt. The thought dismayed her sluggish mind so much that she didn't notice her surroundings until she was settled at a corner of the table and he had left to fetch the food. It was intimately set for two. Three candles burned in a silver candelabrum, the wax which sculpted their slender stems telling her they had been lit for some time. A bowl of richly scented velvety red roses sat beneath them. The plates were fluted with gold, the scrolled silver cutlery gleaming lustrously in the candlelight. A glass of red wine and half-empty bottle next to Lucas's setting told its own story. Somehow the image of Lucas, sitting alone at the graceful table, sipping his wine and watching the candles burn as he waited for...her?...was achingly poignant. After the sad farewell she had just attended it felt, to her unutterable confusion, like a warm and wonderful welcome.

'Did you do this just for me?' she murmured when he wheeled in a serving trolley and began to ladle a creamy, steaming soup into delicate white and gold bowls. 'Surely not; you didn't even know when I'd be back...'

The fate note of yearning in her whisky-mellowed voice didn't escape him. He set the soup before her.

'Eat,' he ordered as he sat down and followed his own command. He talked of inconsequential things, and accepted her tentative compliments on his cooking with comfortable ease. He teased her and made her laugh for the first time in days. Lulled into a false sense of security by his lazy air and lack of aggression, the light, yet satisfyingly filling food he had prepared and single glass of wine he allowed her, Victoria found herself wrapped in a delicious haze of forgetful well-being. After a frothy dessert concoction which he unashamedly admitted he had bought from a local gourmet store Victoria happily floated into the big lounge where she found, to her childish delight, that he had lit a fire.

'Oh, I love fires!' she cried, kneeling down in front of it to enjoy the flow of heat with a sensuous pleasure that wasn't at all childish.

'I thought you might.' He watched her tilt her head to feel the glowing caress on her bare throat. In her prim black dress she looked like a passionate Puritan, and his loins tightened as she turned and gave him a mock-stern look that enhanced the contradictory image.

'It's not really cold enough for fires yet. It's not even autumn,' she scolded half-heartedly. 'You really shouldn't have.'

'If I never did anything I shouldn't I'd never get anywhere,' he murmured cryptically, handing her a cup of
coffee.

'Mmm.' She ran her tongue dreamily over the foam
on her lips as she sipped. 'How come I have to do the
cooking round here when you can make a simple coffee
taste like this?'

'Because it's not just simple coffee,' he said, sitting
down beside her on the thick carpet. She was so relaxed
that she was practically fluid. She was also looking at
him with big, dark, unknowingly wistful eyes. He could
feel himself begin to sweat like an adolescent. So much
for the suave seducer. Anticipation had made him as hard
as a rock and he was having difficulty in stringing two
thoughts together that didn't involve her howling with
pleasure in his arms. But he was damned if he was going
to make a move before she completed her own seduction. It was a matter of personal pride. 'It's got
Frangelico in it, and whipped cream, and one or two
spices.'

'It's lovely,' Victoria sighed, inhaling the fragrance of
the almond-flavoured liqueur. She drained her cup and
put it down on the stone hearth and then gave in to a
sensuous impulse and stretched out full length on her
side, staring into the flames.

There was a long silence behind her and at last she
rolled over on to her back and looked at Lucas through
lowered lashes. She was slightly irritated when he didn't
look back. He continued to stare across her into the fire,
as if she wasn't even there. One knee was drawn up, the
other leg lying bent beneath it. The hand resting across
his raised knee was relaxed, the other braced behind him,
supporting the backward slant of his torso. The loose
white shirt had no collar but was buttoned to the throat
and gathered softly at his shoulders and wrists. The
flowing, shapeless silk cloaked the hard male lines of his
body and yet somehow seemed to emphasise rather than
defuse his aura of masculinity. The overall effect was
disturbingly romantic. He looked broodingly tough and
fascinatingly sexy, so warm and so very alive...Victoria's

gaze drifted to his mouth, and the line between reality and fantasy suddenly blurred because his mouth was coming closer...

It touched her heavy eyelids, one after the other, pressing them closed with a gentle insistence to which she dreamily succumbed. In the safe, warm, velvety blackness her desire was teased by the soft, moist tugging at her lower lip. He bit her mouth and her lips parted, he bit her tongue and she moaned, but not from hurt. The fire was no longer in the hearth, but inside her. The reality of the touch and taste and smell of him was more than she could deny.

She opened her eyes. His were closed, his thick brows drawn together as he voluptuously explored her mouth. His expression was almost one of pain but, if so, she knew his pain was deliberately self-inflicted. She suddenly had a vivid picture of what he was doing and it made her liquid with desire. He was pleasuring himself on her, using her submissive mouth to slowly build himself to a peak of arousal. He wasn't hurried. He wasn't intent on forcing a response. He was simply...enjoying himself. There was no sense of urgency. If she wanted him to stop, he would, but...if she wanted to enjoy herself, too, well...there was no one, nothing, to stop her now. The knowledge was heady, arousing.

She put her hands on his upper arms, felt the hard bridge of muscle that supported him over her. She wanted to feel that hardness against her. She tugged. His eyes opened...hot, dark, glittering. His mouth lifted, slowly, as his body sank down, obedient to her silent urging, a hard thigh pushing between her legs, his chest creating a tight, crushing pressure over her aching breasts. He moved his big body on hers, grinding her softly, sensuously into the carpet, watching her face with a greedy triumph that she was too bewildered with pleasure to resent. She felt a tight congestion in her belly. Everything seemed to be happening in slow motion and she suddenly felt a surge of fear that there wouldn't be enough time, that, as always before, that bright, distant

destination would fade before she got there. She plunged
her hands into the thick, soft dark hair and pulled his
head down, fighting him for possession of the moment.
He meekly followed her lead, pulling her on to her side
so that his hands could slide unhindered to her breasts,
shaping the roundness beneath the stiff fabric as she ravished his mouth with a touchingly inexpert hunger. She
couldn't get enough of him and she began to shake with
the frustration as he tried to soothe her.

'Ssh, it's all right, slow down, darling...' he teased,
stilling her feverish shivers with his body. 'Don't rush
me...we'll get there...'

'When?' Her plaintive cry was swallowed by his lavish
kiss as he picked her up and held her high against his
chest. 'Where are you taking me?'

'To bed. Where you belong——'

'But I don't want to go to bed. I want to stay here
with you—I'm not tired, I'm not drunk, either.' She
arched against his hold, terrified he was going to use her
own weakness against her.

He held her easily. 'I know you're not...' His smile
was gloriously savage.

He put her down in the lift and kissed her all the way
up to the first floor and then, when she would have
stepped out of the open door, pulled her back against
his chest, his hands cupping her black-clad breasts as he
turned her.

'Look,' he murmured, and she saw them in the infinity of mirrors, fully dressed and yet poised in the very
act of love, the possessive male and the wanton woman.
They were both breathing raggedly, their faces flushed,
their mouths ripely red. As she looked his hands moved
under her breasts, lifting and tightening in a gesture of
explicit sexuality.

'Soon my mouth will be here...and here...' Slowly
and provocatively his hands slid down over her belly to
make a V against the juncture of her thighs, his palms
pressing against the warm feminine mound, his fingers
curving, lightly pressing inwards and up. She shuddered,
her hips helplessly straining to his touch as he nudged

himself insistently against her soft buttocks. The stark reflection of their flagrant lust should have shocked her. It didn't. They looked as if they belonged together. As if her body was made expressly to accommodate his, two halves of a whole. All that mattered now was being allowed to give the love and passion she had so long suppressed its fullest and finest expression....

In his room Lucas undressed her slowly, admiring her with his eyes, his hands, his mouth...and she felt no embarrassment, only bloomed under his erotic reverence. He made her undress him...and she felt no shyness, only stunning awe as his muscles shivered under her touch. This time she didn't have to fight the dizzying joy of watching his naked body move and bend and flex...it was her right. This time there would be no doors closing, only new ones opening, drawing her on to heady new experiences.

He was already hugely aroused and for one disconcerting moment as he drew her down into the silken depths of the huge, sunken bed she was aware of a vague ache of loss, bordering on disappointment. There was no need now for games, or for pretence. He didn't have to stimulate her with whispers of passion, or slow caresses; he knew she was already trembling at the brink of fulfilment. All it was going to take was one thrust of that powerful body and she would drown in bliss...

She was in a feverish agony of need and yet, as he parted her thighs, Victoria experienced a fleeting premonition of *tristesse*. Soon, too soon, it would be all over...

CHAPTER NINE

A DISTANT vibration disturbed Victoria in her cosy cocoon. She frowned, cuddling back against the animal warmth that was the source of her contentment, only vaguely aware of the unaccustomed weight on her hip that was dislodged with her movement.

Victoria's eyes fluttered open in shock as she felt the warm weight resolve itself into a seeking hand. Daylight shafted through the half-open vertical blinds, golden stripes on the floor arrowing towards the sunken bed. The hand settled on her breast, conforming firmly and familiarly around the soft mound. A hard forearm pressed against her breastbone, an elbow curved over the dip in her waist. A thick, hairy thigh pushed lazily in between hers, completing the encirclement, binding her securely to the soft bed. Against the long line of her back she could feel the brush of a dense, soft, furry pelt.

Lucas.

Victoria's drowsiness vanished, her breast tingling to life in the warm cup of his palm. Her body felt sensuously heavy, throbbing faintly with a pleasant, all-over ache that wasn't surprising considering the intensive exercise that she had been engaged in. How naïve she had been indeed, to think that Lucas's passion would be swiftly assuaged. He had spent all night showing her differently. And that first time hadn't been the quick, lusty coupling she had expected, either. Once he had her down among his exotic sheets and cushions Lucas's erotic urgency had abruptly left him. He had become almost playful, tender, teasing her feverishly sensitive skin with the rough magic of his body hair, touching and tasting her delicately for a long time before he had eased between her thighs. In spite of her readiness, she had been very, very tight and they had both stilled instantly, breathless, staring at each other while her body had adjusted to the swollen fullness of him.

'Am I hurting you?' he had groaned thickly, his whole body rigid with restraint.

'A little—no!' Her body tightened around him as he withdrew slightly and he groaned again, a guttural, helpless sound that made her gasp. 'No...please...I like it——' She almost fainted at the exquisite, dragging pleasure his tiny movement had generated. It was such an incredible understatement that she blushed wildly under his slitted stare. His hips moved again, slowly, experimentally, and she arched and twisted to try and prolong the delicious momentum of his gentle thrust. She felt rather than saw the rippling contractions that shivered across his belly and braced thighs as her soft body welcomed its satin-hard invader with deep contractions of its own. The small rhythmic undulations had been like an explosive trigger. Suddenly he was the arrogant, conquering hero carving a place for himself inside her, moving harder, faster, deeper, stretching and filling her until the hard bones of his pelvis ground against hers, possessing her to the hilt with a hoarse shout of fierce gratification. He had possessed her so completely that there had been no room for any doubts or regrets, no room for anything but the relentless quest for the next peak of pleasure...and the next. It had been a shattering introduction into the unexplored depths of her own sexuality. It had never been like that with Joshua...

Joshua.

Victoria covered her mouth to stop the small cry of horror that welled up in her throat, the cold metal of her wedding-ring pressing into her swollen lips. Joshua was dead and instead of mourning his loss she had...*celebrated*, falling into bed with her lover at the first opportunity! She felt sick with shame. What kind of person was she, had she become? She had let everyone down—Joshua, David, Lucas...but most of all herself. Her reckless irresponsibility sent chills up her spine. Fortunately Lucas had been prepared, but the idea of contraception hadn't even entered Victoria's head. And if it had, she had the awful suspicion that she wouldn't have cared. In fact, the thought of Lucas giving her a baby of his to love made her feel warm and cosy inside. With a muffled cry of shame she began to edge out from under the heavy male limbs. What had she *done*...?

Last night she had admitted unequivocally to herself that she loved Lucas. For weeks she had been fiercely resisting the knowledge, but now there was no going back. So why did she feel even more alienated from herself than ever? Because she wasn't loved in return, her heart replied. Because Lucas had had ample time to tell her that he loved her, but he hadn't. Because Lucas was honest. Lucas was frank and unashamed of his physical needs. Lucas was everything she wasn't and she didn't deserve his love...

The arm over her breastbone contracted suddenly and a low grumble vibrated against her shoulder-blades. Her hopes of slipping away unnoticed were banished when, after a discreetly brief wrestle she found her nose buried in a hairy chest. She tipped her head up to find Lucas regarding her with sleepy satisfaction. 'Morning, sweetheart...'

Victoria's reply was lost in his leisurely kiss. Sweetheart. The way he said that, he almost made her believe it... She panicked.

'I've got to get up——' She squirmed backwards, so at least her belly wasn't crushed against his overt maleness.

'I was just having a rather lovely dream,' he murmured into her ear as her mouth evaded his.

'What about?' she gasped, naïvely thinking to distract him.

He laughed, his hands tangling with hers as she tried to fend him off. 'I dreamt that I woke up to find you naked in my bed.'

Oh, God. 'Lucas——'

She didn't have to try and think up another distraction. She suddenly became aware that the distant vibration that had woken her had been the arrival of a car. Now she could hear a very familiar voice floating up the stairs, nearing rapidly.

She sat up abruptly, dragging the sheet against her breasts.

'Lucas, it's David.' She stared, aghast, at the door, half expecting it to crash open.

'And Gabby. He's probably come over to see her. Relax, Victoria.' Lucas bent and grabbed several cushions and stuffed them behind him, flaunting his magnificent chest as he leaned back, folding his hands behind his head, studying her flustered face and the freckled shoulders that he now knew intimately, freckle by delicious freckle.

Relax! 'At this time of the morning! No, he's here to see me——' Just as Jason had predicted. Victoria wondered how she was going to climb out of the sleeping pit without utterly discarding what remained of her modesty.

'It's ten o'clock,' Luke pointed out lazily.

Victoria was horrified. 'I've never stayed in bed that late in my life!'

'I'm flattered,' murmured Lucas in throaty amusement. 'What other things did you do in bed with me that you've never done before?'

Victoria went scarlet and he laughed. 'That many, huh?'

'I've got to get out of here.' She wrenched the sheet away from where it had become tucked under his solid hip and wrapped it fully around her as she half backed, half rolled up out of the bed. Lucas made no move to stop her. He simply lay there, stark naked, amused, aroused.

Victoria froze as she heard David and Gabby pass the bedroom, and she caught the gist of their words, Gabby saying, '...my own breakfast...didn't answer when I called...'

And David, his voice firmly adamant. '...Won't mind...yesterday...said some things....' His voice faded towards Victoria's room and she was galvanised into action.

She snatched up her underwear and struggled to put it on under the sheet.

'For goodness' sake, stop looking so guilty, darling, he's not your husband——' said Lucas, unknowingly twisting the knife.

Victoria's hands shook badly as she jerked up the zip on her mourning dress. Lucas swore. He leaped out of the bed and Victoria shied, but he only sent her a grimly mocking look as he moved past her to the long wardrobe. He slid his arms into his short, black silk robe, turning as he belted it.

'Calm down, Victoria, I'm not going to leap on you. But we are going to have a talk——'

Victoria's gaze jerked past him to fasten on the door. She could hear David again, his voice pitched more urgently this time.

'Last night...upset...would she go——?'

And Gabby answering with awful clarity, 'I don't know. Dad and I didn't get in until late ourselves. Lucas was here, though.' There was a light, rapid tattoo on the door. 'Luke? Are you awake?'

It was Victoria's worst nightmare come to life. She dived for the concealed bathroom door but Lucas caught her by the arm and whirled her around to face him.

'Let me go. You can't let them see us.'

Her frantic whisper infuriated him. 'Why not? I've done nothing to be ashamed of.' He began hauling her with him towards the door.

'But *I* have,' Victoria blurted wildly.

'By making love with me?' he asked smboulderingly.

'We didn't make love.' She mustn't want what she couldn't have. 'We had——'

'Don't say it, Victoria,' he cut savagely across her denial. 'Don't you dare! He's put you up on a pedestal, a cold, lonely pedestal. It's time to come down. It's time that everyone realises that you're just a flesh-and-blood woman——'

And with that he threw open the door.

Victoria didn't know who was more shocked, herself or Gabby and David. She saw David's bloodshot eyes fall to her crumpled dress, the dress she had worn the evening before. She saw him look at Lucas, obviously just out of bed, and the possessive hold that flaunted the truth. Gabby, the hard-nosed, soignée business-woman, actually blushed.

'I came to apologise,' David said in a slow, stunned voice. 'But I see I needn't have bothered...'

'David, it isn't what you think——'

'Yes, it is,' said Lucas brutally. 'It's exactly what he thinks. We're lovers.'

David rocked on his heels but he didn't say anything. To Victoria his sober, haggard silence was more damning than his drunken anger of the day before.

'Only since last night,' blundered Victoria wretchedly, only making things worse.

'Last *night*?' David looked sick. 'My God, Tory, couldn't you have waited a bit longer? At least until Dad was cold in his grave!'

Fresh shame overwhelmed Victoria. It was true, she had behaved like a wanton, her greedy passion an ob-scene codicil to Joshua's quiet passing.

'How long is long enough, for God's sake?' Lucas demanded harshly. 'Do you expect Victoria to wear widow's weeds forever?'

'Not forever, no,' said David wearily. 'But certainly longer than a few days...'

'But your father was killed *years* ago.' Gabby found her voice.

'He didn't die in that accident,' said David flatly. 'He's been in a coma. He died three days ago. The funeral was yesterday. Victoria has been a widow for less than a week...'

The words flowed out of him like a flood. He wasn't destroying her through deliberate malice, Victoria re-alised numbly, but because her fall from grace had ap-parently freed his own imprisoned conscience to speak. There in the hallway he had made peace with himself at last, accepting the wisdom of the words that he had spoken, but not yet believed in his heart, the day before—the proud eulogy that had been his last gift to his father.

When he had gone, trailing a bewildered Gabby in his wake, Victoria had wanted to crawl into her room and hide, but she couldn't.

Although Lucas had let her arm go some time during David's painful confession his cold stare was manacle enough. He was looking at her as if he had never seen her before. And because of her deception he hadn't, not really.

'Were you thinking of him?' At her blank stare he snarled, 'When you were moaning in my arms, were you pretending I was your husband?'

'Of course not!'

Her genuine horror didn't impress him in the least.

'So what was I? A fling to celebrate your freedom? Your initiation back into the singles' club——?'

'*No!*' To poison herself with that thought had been bad enough, but to have him do it was unbearable. 'Lucas—you must believe me, last night was nothing to do with Joshua——'

'The hell it wasn't!' Dark colour flared across the hard cheekbones, his black eyes bitter. 'It had *everything* to do with him. And *nothing* to do with me. You made sure of that. You made sure that we were never anything but strangers. Maybe in some sick way you enjoyed the intrigue of it all. You knew I thought you were free...I let you see how I felt. While *you*...!' His disgust changed to an expression of utter self-loathing. 'I *trusted* you...I tied myself in knots trying to reconcile my protective instincts with my baser urges, going slowly with you so as not to offend your moral dignity. I thought you were being shy when you were just manipulating me. I even thought——' His shoulder muscles bunched under the thin black silk as he savagely mastered his revulsion. '*God,* what a fool I must have seemed!'

'I never thought you were a fool,' she said desperately. 'Lucas, when I came here I never wanted to—never expected to...to...' Fall in love...

'Get hoist with your own petard?' His smouldering rage burst out again into a fiery blaze. 'You might have kidded yourself you were being faithful, but as far as

I'm concerned you weren't faithful to either of us. You used us both in your sordid little charade. You used the secret of his existence to keep *me* at bay and you used me to ease the frustrations of a spurious widowhood, because you couldn't have *him* . . .'

'No, I was confused——'

'You *lied*.'

'Yes, yes, I lied,' she admitted wildly. 'But only because——'

'Because you wanted sex without emotional intimacy.'

The contemptuous statement had such a cutting edge of truth that Victoria was slashed to the bone. She had known from the start that no real relationship could be built on a lie, but she had blinded herself to the consequences. In acting against her nature she had destroyed her own integrity and threatened his. No wonder Lucas despised her. She had no defence against his contempt.

'I didn't deliberately lead you on. I tried *not* to get involved,' she pointed out wretchedly.

'If you had really wanted to say no, all you had to do was mention the three magic words: "I'm still married",' he ground out. 'But you played coy. You wanted what happened to happen. Your doe-eyed reluctance was an invitation in itself. What man wouldn't have followed you into temptation? Damn you, I actually admired you for your gentleness and vulnerability, but you're about as vulnerable as steel. You don't need me any more than I need you——'

What man . . . he said that as if she would have responded to any man in the way she had to him, and he to any woman, as if it had just been a male-female game they had played—and she had broken the unwritten rules of play. The fatal wound had been to his pride, not his heart.

'In that case you won't object if I resign,' she said quietly, but instead of seizing the opportunity to get rid of her she found that she had presented him with the perfect revenge.

'If you think you're going to walk away that easily, think again,' he said with a savagely humourless smile.

'You're not going to leave Dad in the lurch just because you want to enjoy your new status. You seem to be conveniently forgetting that you signed an employment contract agreeing to a fortnight's notice on either side. At least Iris should be back by then. You are going to abide by the terms, aren't you? Or are you a cheat as well as a liar? If so, you can do your own dirty work. *You* can tell Dad...'

He knew he had her. Whatever her other failings, her over-developed sense of duty would never let her betray anyone weaker than herself. Perhaps, thought Lucas grimly, if he had sought to evoke her compassion rather than her passion, he could have clawed out a place for himself in her entrenched loyalties. But that would have made him as much a liar as she. He was a strong man, and always dealt from his strength rather than his weaknesses. It was galling to discover that what he had considered his strengths—his self-confidence and determination—had led him astray, and his greatest asset, his brilliant brain, had been as easily conned as his emotions.

In the back of his mind he had sometimes disloyally wondered how his wise and warm mother could have been so stupid as to fall victim to his natural father's calculated charm. Now he knew. It was all too easy to devoutly believe only what you wanted to believe. Even cynics were apparently not immune. Human logic was ever at the mercy of the senses. For instance, at this moment his genius was completely immobilised by virulent jealousy—of a dead man. He felt even more betrayed by Joshua West's recent death than by the discovery that, up until a few days ago, Victoria's husband had still been alive! At least if Victoria had given herself to Lucas while her husband still lived it would have given him *some* hope. It would have meant that her feelings for Lucas were too powerful for her to control, strong enough to overcome any moral or physical obstacles in the path of their relationship. Although the idea of engaging in adultery, even unwittingly, was repugnant, in the tragic circumstances he might have eventually been able to reconcile himself to taking second place in her loyalties, if not her affections. As it was, she had given him nothing but her body last night. She had withheld from him everything else of importance. She had gone with him to the brink of paradise and then flung him effortlessly into the black pit of hell, and now she was proposing to walk away and leave him there, alone. To her beloved Joshua she had freely offered a lifetime of devoted care, no matter what the personal cost to herself. Lucas was only worthy of the dregs. His anger rose like a black tide in his throat.

If he had to endure the bitter hell of rejection, then he damned well wasn't going to do it alone!

Victoria had thought that the previous few days were the worst of her life but she was soon to change her mind. She had hoped that Lucas would bring his formidable intelligence to bear on the situation once he had calmed down, but, instead of softening, his bitter contempt seemed to harden and seek new outlets with each passing day. He continued to work at home in his study, to demand his regular infusions of coffee and his meals at his desk. Whenever Victoria went into the room she could feel the temperature drop by ten degrees. And the way he watched her was unnerving, that dark, unwinking stare following her every move, silent, brooding and openly mistrustful. Her hands would tremble as she poured out his coffee and he would smile that hard, satisfied smile that told her more clearly than words that he saw through her attempted indifference. He was deliberately tormenting her and there wasn't a thing she could do about it without betraying her heart. If he guessed that she had fallen in love with him he would despise her even more. What value was the love of a dishonourable woman? She deserved his contempt and thus she must suffer the penance for her shameful sin.

Scott, at least, seemed more hurt than upset that she hadn't confided in him.

'Did you think I wouldn't understand? Of all people, I would be the most *likely* to understand. I know what it's like to feel trapped. To seek to deny what undeniably *is.* I would never have imposed the burden of my compassion on you...'

'I know. I'm sorry, Scott.' Victoria had been further shattered by his concern. 'I just didn't want to jeopardise my chances of the job... and then, when David gave you all the impression that Joshua had been killed in the accident, I... I just couldn't face explaining it all. I don't think David would have forgiven me at that time if I'd exposed his feelings about his father...' So she'd sacrificed Lucas's forgiveness instead.

'Have you told Lucas this?'

Victoria looked away, her throat constricting. 'I tried. I—he wouldn't listen.'

She had tried twice, but Lucas had cut her off with a verbal slap in the face. She didn't think she could survive a third rejection—her self-respect was already in brittle fragments—so she had taken refuge in the stoic reserve which had sustained her so well over the years. Only this time she had discovered her resources of strength severely depleted.

Scott said gently, not needing further explanation, 'Give him time. Lucas sets high standards for himself and he's developed a taste for being in control. He's so rarely wrong, you see. With his brain he doesn't often find himself in a situation he hasn't predicted and therefore isn't prepared for. It's a new experience for him. Maybe he needs to come to terms with his own sense of failure before he can try and see things from your point of view. It's because he cares for you that he's so upset. It's easier to forgive an enemy than to forgive a friend...'

Or a lover. A breach of faith between lovers was tantamount to infidelity. If she suddenly discovered now that Lucas had a wife, or even ex-wife lurking somewhere in the background, Victoria knew she would feel utterly devastated. It was *her* failure, not Lucas's, that he was paying for.

'I don't blame Lucas. He's been perfectly innocent in all of this mess...'

To her reproachful surprise Scott laughed at that. 'Lucas is not a perfect anything. And I think even he would be insulted if you called him innocent. But I think that maybe he did expect *you* to be perfect...'

Victoria remembered what Lucas said about her coming down off her pedestal. She was down with a vengeance, and it did seem to be only Lucas who hadn't adjusted to the swift disillusionment. Gabby had been more fascinated and admiring of her spirit than condemning, and even David had behaved with impeccable discretion since the day of the funeral. When she had bravely faced her family to let them know that she had resigned from her job David had been the first to console Victoria with the bracing thought that she would soon find another. They had all offered to help. No one mentioned Lucas, and that uncharacteristic incuriosity had been a dead giveaway, especially in the girls. David had warned them off. Victoria was deeply embarrassed by their knowing concern, and touched by their lack of condemnation.

Lucas more than made up for their lack. Although he was at home all day to haunt her, at night he had suddenly plunged into a mad social whirl—on each occasion bringing a different woman home for a 'nightcap'—none of them his goddaughter! On the first occasion Victoria had been caught totally off guard by his early return. Lucas had insisted on dragging his bemused date into the kitchen to introduce her. She had been tall and willowy and beautiful in the very classical blonde sense. Victoria, in a floury apron, sweaty and flushed from the baking she had been doing to take her mind off her troubles had been stricken, as no doubt Lucas intended her to be. As he guided his guest back to the drawing-room he paused to request that Victoria bring them both one of her special spiced coffees before she retired for the night. Her eyes had flashed at him and he had said softly, lethally mocking, 'Sour grapes, Victoria? I would have thought that it would suit your martyr complex to serve your replacement...'

Pride had dictated that she serve the cosy twosome with a dignified deference but afterwards, in the lonely sanctuary of her luxurious room, she had wept for what might have been.

Only it turned out that the classical beauty hadn't been her replacement, for the next night it had been a different woman, and the next. Victoria knew exactly what he was doing. He was showing her that she had just been one in a string of unimportant one-night stands.

On the morning that a photograph of Lucas and the previous night's lady of choice, a university professor who could have doubled for Marilyn Monroe, appeared in the newspaper Victoria was viciously pleased to note that Lucas was in the throes of a violent hangover. So he had to get drunk now to enjoy himself, did he? She set his usual cooked breakfast in front of him and watched him blanch. When he pushed it away, demanding a hair of the dog, she couldn't help saying in a nasty whisper, 'Don't you mean a hair of the *bitch*?'

Lucas gave her a bloodshot stare, glancing at Scott buried comfortably behind his morning paper before he murmured sardonically, 'Jealous, Cinders?'

'Why should I be? *You're* not my prince,' she clipped back.

His slightly grey face went one shade paler, his mouth tightening unevenly, his eyes growing stormy, and she realised that he thought she was taunting him with Joshua. She had spoken impulsively but she didn't try to disabuse him. She, who had never deliberately hurt anyone in her life, was discovering that love and passion had its dark side, a side that took pleasure in inflicting and bearing pain. She might be in agony but she had never felt more alive in her life as when she was loving or hating Lucas. She was bewildered by the emergence of herself as a woman that she hardly even recognised. A woman filled with anger, with violent and uncomfortable emotions struggling to find expression.

'I never said I was,' he said grimly, when he had his flaring temper under control. 'You're the one who played a masquerade. I'll be in for dinner tonight, by the way... with a guest.'

Victoria went rigid, but she was saved from further humiliation by Gabby's cheerful good morning as she pulled out a chair.

'A guest tonight? Who?'

'Nicole Blackburn.' Lucas spoke to his sister, but his eyes were on Victoria's strained face.

Gabby's eyebrows rose as she sat down and helped herself to coffee. '*Another* one? What are you trying to prove with this parade of lovelies, Luke? That you can't find a woman you can bear to spend more than a single night with?'

It was so accurate a shot that Lucas flushed, and Gabby felt justified in goading her brother further. He really was acting like a prize idiot!

'I know variety is the spice and all that, but I hope you're practising safe sex, Luke. I mean, all these sophisticated swingers you've suddenly developed a taste for... you don't know where they've been——'

Scott lowered his paper, saying only a mildly reproachful, 'Gabrielle!' as Lucas exploded.

'Who I go out with and what I do with them is none of your damned business! Do I ask *you* if you're sleeping with David?'

'No, but since we've been seriously talking marriage I suppose you've drawn your own conclusions,' said Gabby outrageously. 'I don't suppose you're thinking of marrying any of your stable——'

'Enjoying the company of attractive women doesn't make me a rutting stallion,' Lucas snarled violently. 'I don't sleep with every woman I meet and nor do I want to. I do have a brain, you know; some women find that even more appealing than my body.' He broke off and cast a savagely accusing look at Victoria, as if she had been the interrogator who had dragged that revealing confession from the depths of his frustration.

So he wasn't sleeping with any of them. Strangely, the knowledge gave Victoria no joy. The time would come when he *would* find a woman far more suited to his physical and intellectual needs than Victoria could ever hope to be. It might seem an eternity to her, but in reality it wouldn't be long before a man as brilliant and determined as Lucas worked all the hostility out of his system and regained his sense of proportion. Perhaps then he would cease to lash her with his hatred.

Victoria, back in the kitchen where no thoughts of inferiority haunted her, decided that she would prepare something stunningly elaborate for dinner, just to prove that she wasn't sickeningly jealous of the intellectually curious Nicole!

She had hardly begun culling her cookery book when the phone rang. Iris's cousin, it appeared, had vanished in answer to a plea for help from another branch of the family and Iris was getting bored. She had decided she felt well enough to return to work and, Iris being Iris, there was to be no hanging about. Doctor's certificate in hand, she expected to be back in harness on the morrow!

All thoughts of the elaborate dinner evaporated as the realisation slammed into Victoria. Lucas had told her she had to stay until Iris returned. From tomorrow she would be free of all her obligations. No meals to prepare, no hospital to visit, no Scott to entertain—he was so independent now, he hardly needed her anyway.

It was not just a page in her life she would turn tomorrow; she would be starting a whole new volume. She could do anything she wanted with the rest of her life. There would be no guilty secrets to hold her back, no chains of duty to bind her ambition. Tracey and Maxine were due to fly back to Sydney in a few days, David was all wrapped up in the fresh beginning of a totally open relationship with Gabrielle, and Jason was buried to his ears in exams and, ironically, a rapidly developing friendship with Tanya Jacobson. For the first time in years no one was relying on Victoria. Freedom, now that she had it well and truly within her grasp, was utterly frightening...and excruciatingly lonely...

She decided on the ubiquitous prawn cocktail and a simple casserole followed by an easy dessert and then whisked around the house to make sure that there were no glaring oversights that Iris could pounce on as evidence that she should never dare have another illness. Then she went quietly to her room to pack.

She cleared the wardrobe of most of her clothes and was just taking out the dark green dress, wistfully smoothing its beautiful folds, when she heard a breath of sound behind her.

'Scott told me that Iris rang.'

'Yes.' Victoria thrust the green dress hastily into her suitcase and closed it, not looking at Lucas in case he should see the betraying sheen in her eyes.

'So you're walking out, just like that?'

Her head jerked up at the harsh demand, her tears vanquished by anger. 'Not until tomorrow. I'll be here to serve your damned dinner!'

'The hell with dinner! God, you just can't wait to leave, can you?' He stepped into the room, filling it with his crackling tension.

'I thought you wanted me to go...' Years of her life had been expended in broken hopes. She wasn't going to waste any more of her precious store of dreams.

'Since when has what *I* want figured so highly in your desires?'

That last sarcastic word slid under her fragile defences and she shivered at the images it evoked. He stilled, arrested by the tiny movement. The tension in him shifted, grew. He moved closer and she stepped back, almost stumbling over the suitcase she had thrust on the floor.

'Don't——'

'Don't what? You're always saying that—"don't", "no", "I can't"... But you can, and did, didn't you, Victoria? When it comes down to it, the words don't mean a thing. You're no different from me. You have appetites and they hunger to be fed. I satisfied you that night, didn't I, darling? You couldn't get enough of me.' He taunted her with the knowledge of their shared weakness. 'Care for another little...stimulation of our palates...?'

He touched her arm, just lightly, and it was like a blow across her heart. She couldn't speak for the pain of his caress. His fingers tightened around her wrist and he pulled her roughly into him. She gasped. He was hot and hard and brutally sure.

'I was the first man for you, wasn't I, Victoria?'

'I don't know what you——'

He gave her a short, sharp nudge with his hips and rasped gloatingly, 'You told me you'd never felt that way in bed before. Joshua couldn't do it for you, even though you loved him. I wasn't your first lover, but I was the first man to show you what you're capable of. I was your first extra-marital experience. Your first *lover* ... And I gave you your first taste of pure ecstasy, your first climax ...' He hadn't needed to be told, he had seen and felt her shuddering fear and wonder as her body had stormed out of control, and now he used his knowledge ruthlessly. 'You owe me ...'

He kissed her, a kiss as savagely challenging as his words, his tongue stopping her feverish protest. She struggled, he subdued her; she arched away from him, he followed; she writhed, he groaned with pleasure. He forced her to the bed and straddled her, his hands seeking and intimately exploiting her responses, shaping the nature of her struggles to satisfy their mutual need as he stripped the clothes from her with ruthless speed, and shrugged free of his own. She was shamingly aware that the close, desperate tussle had aroused her as much it had him. Her breasts grew ripe and swollen under his insolent caresses, the stiff peaks aching for the attention of his wandering mouth. When he began to suckle moistly she cried out, drawing her legs together to hide the extent of her excitement at his brutal seduction, but the perfume of her arousal betrayed her. Lucas wove skilful fingers between the imprisoning walls of silky-tender thighs and knew as he found her that her resistance was only skin-deep. Inside she was melting for him. Yet still she refused to accept the inevitable. But she would ... he would *make* her accept everything he had to offer!

At the last minute he forced himself to hold back.

'Shall I stop now, Victoria?' he taunted her hoarsely. 'If you want me to stop now, I will...'

She couldn't. Her love and longing were too great to deny, and to her eternal, dizzy gratitude he didn't linger over the finer points of her submission, he took it arrogantly, passionately, as his rightful due.

'Tell me what you're feeling...' he growled thickly as he moved powerfully between her thighs. 'Talk to me, damn you, tell me what I do to you...'

'You know...'

'I know but I want to hear it all the same. I'm inside you, I'm a part of your essence. Lie to me now, Victoria. Tell me I have nothing to offer you when I can give you *this*...and *this*...' With each thrust he drove deeper behind the barrier of her reserve. 'Tell me you couldn't ever love me the way you loved *him*...tell me you don't want more of me than this single...moment of...supreme...*sensation*!' His hard body strained and shuddered as he fought against an early release in order to prolong the pleasure. His hard face clenched, his eyes closing, his strong back arching as his hips slammed into hers, his last words coming as a ragged shout as he thrust them both violently to the top of the peak and over the edge. 'Dammit, Victoria, give *in*! I love you, what the hell more can you ask?'

CHAPTER TEN

VICTORIA paid off the taxi driver with the last of her cash and turned to face the big old house. The late afternoon sun laid bare its shabbiness with slanting precision. Home. For once the appellation brought no wistful rush of memories.

Victoria picked up her suitcase and walked towards the front steps, feeling her new shoes pinch a little. Not only her shoes were new. A different Victoria had emerged during her three-week holiday, a glossy, smartly dressed Victoria with a fashionably feathered haircut.

For the first time in her life Victoria had freely lavished money on herself. She had bought whatever she fancied, eaten out in restaurants, taken sightseeing tours and generally behaved like a frivolous tourist. The small nest-egg of Joshua's life insurance pay-out, which she had formerly intended to sensibly invest, had been scattered heedlessly by her normally thrifty fingers. She refused to regret one moment of her fling, even though the experience had not been entirely pleasant. For, all the while that she was pretending to be heart-whole and fancy free, Victoria had felt a deep well of loneliness growing inside her. In spite of her reserve she was not, she had discovered, solitary by nature. Certainly she had desperately needed the rest, the escape, but now she could no longer keep the unanswered questions from beating at her brain.

Did Lucas really love her, or had he just been saying what he'd thought she needed to hear? At the end of that passionate encounter in her bedroom, instead of holding her trembling body in his arms and tenderly reiterating his vow of love, Lucas had scrambled up and dressed with indecent haste, scarcely able to bring himself to look at her as he apologised tautly for his attack. And then he had fled as if afraid that she might hold him to his word. Victoria had finished packing her bag before walking out the door in a daze.

When she had arrived home a message from Dr Martin was waiting. The parents of the young woman who had received Joshua's liver had offered his widow the use of their holiday home in Queenstown, a scenic paradise in the South Island, as a gesture of sympathy and gratitude. Victoria's decision to go there by herself had stunned everyone, including herself, but the bolt-hole was too timely to ignore. She had never been away on holiday, let alone by herself, but she hadn't given herself time for her resolve to falter. She had booked her seat on the airline—flying would be another first—and been gone by the following day.

She had behaved impulsively by running away, but it had been an act of self-preservation. Lucas had very graphically demonstrated that the physical attraction between them was too strong for her to deny but, no matter how desperately she wanted him, Victoria would never consent to an affair without a deep emotional commitment on both sides. And, although she loved him, the prospect of making that commitment petrified her.

Victoria didn't think she could bear to go through the cycle of love, fear, anger, pain and loss all over again. If Lucas did love her, how could she love him back as fully and unreservedly as he deserved to be loved, when she felt so strangled by inhibitions?

Victoria used the key from under the flower-pot to open the front door, relieved that there was apparently no one home to make a fuss of her unannounced arrival. She would make herself a cup of tea before she faced up to the reality she had left behind.

She was surprised to notice how tidy the house was as she put down her suitcases and glanced into the living-room on her way to the kitchen. Perhaps Maxine and Tracey had given their brothers a stern lecture about housekeeping before they left, she thought hopefully.

At the door to the kitchen she stopped dead. There, sitting at *her* breakfast bar, drinking from *her* special

mug, and looking every bit at home, was the man who
had occupied so many of her dreams over the past three
weeks.

He looked up and saw her, a calm gesture that showed
how deliberate his air of relaxation was. But his back
stiffened and his eyes narrowed slightly as he took in
her flyaway hair and the leaf-green dress with its daring
neckline and slim skirt. The dress, perfect for the tail-
end of the balmy Auckland summer, was in ultra-fine,
lightweight wool, its gathered shoulders tapering into
tight half-length sleeves that flattered Victoria's slim
arms.

'Welcome home,' he murmured, rising slowly to his
feet. He was wearing a white shirt and black jeans. A
monochrome of masculinity every bit as disturbing as
her vividly coloured dreams. His eyes focused on the
deep V of her neckline. 'Enjoy yourself?'

His mildly lecherous irony made her flush, all her
surface sophistication dissolving into the familiar, vulnerable woman, and the frown that had been forming
between his dark brows turned into a wrinkle of
amusement.

'What are you doing here?' she demanded hastily.

'Would you like some tea? There's still some left in
the pot.'

'Thank you.' How was one supposed to greet an ex-
lover one had run out on? She watched him fossick in
her cupboard and produce another cup. He poured and
handed it to her then sat back down, leaving her standing
like an uninvited guest in her own home. 'You didn't
answer my question.'

'You didn't answer mine,' he replied, pinning her with
that dark, unrevealing stare. 'Did you enjoy yourself in
Queenstown?'

So he *had* known where she was, and still he hadn't
bothered to contact her! Victoria's soft mouth tightened,
her eyes greening defiantly. 'Very much.'

'You look as if you lost a little weight.'

He was staring at her breasts again and to her horror she felt them tingle with anticipation. 'I—got a lot of exercise.'

'What kind of exercise?'

'Not the kind you're thinking about!' she snapped, responding to his look rather than his innocuous enquiry.

'Oh, and what am I thinking about, Victoria?' he murmured, black devils dancing in his eyes. She blushed and he laughed. This wasn't at all how she imagined their next meeting to be. Somehow she had thought that she would be fully in control, calm and dignified while he would be angry and accusing or even humble and pleading.

She set her cup down on the bench with a rattle. 'What are you doing here, Lucas?'

His teasing amusement vanished and Victoria felt the floor tilt under her feet at his grave look. 'I live here.'

'You've been living *here*?'

'Ever since you went away. And I can now fully appreciate why you find the house a burden to keep up. It is rather sprawling for one person to manage, especially when your two co-tenants are so damned messy.'

'You've been living here with David and Jason?' She still couldn't believe it. 'But . . . why?' she whispered.

'Waiting for you to come home. You had to do it some time but you didn't see fit to notify anyone of your timetable.'

'But . . . why *here* . . .?'

'Because this is where you would come first,' he said simply.

'I . . . don't understand . . .'

'That I wanted to be here for you? What's not to understand, Victoria?' he asked holding her steady with his gaze, bewildering her with his gentleness.

'But I . . . aren't you angry?'

'For what? Your going away without telling me? After practically raping you, I didn't have the right to expect anything else. I hoped your time away from me might . . . lessen your fear of me.'

Fear? She stared at him, hearing the note of pain in his voice. She had fears, yes, but none to do with her physical safety. 'You didn't rape me,' she murmured awkwardly.

'But I did. If not physically, then mentally. I deliberately took your choice away from you. What's that if not rape? I have no excuse. I lost my temper. All I knew was that you were leaving me and I couldn't stop you. I'd driven you away with my bull-headed pride and I was furious with myself and furious with you for letting me do it. Dammit, Victoria, you didn't care enough to fight for me. *That* was what destroyed me. It seemed that everyone else deserved your compassionate understanding, your unswerving efforts to heal their wounds except me...except *me!*'

He had started out so beautifully humble and reasonable. Now, as he rose like an avenging spirit before her, she could see the deep intensity that burned in the angry black eyes, splintered with hazel. She stepped back, away from the breathless temptation his passion presented.

'Oh, God, don't be afraid.' The words wrenched from him. 'I'm not going to grab you. That was my mistake in the first place. I sounded like a sulky child just then, didn't I? Everything me, me, *me!* Nothing about what *you've* had to go through...'

He ran a hand through his hair in a gesture of weary distraction. He hadn't shaved that morning and Victoria suddenly noticed that he, too, had lost some weight. It made him look even harder, sexier...

Perhaps she betrayed her thoughts because he said abruptly, 'Those women, Victoria, they were just show. I wanted to hurt you the way that you hurt me, by making you jealous. Never mind that you had just lost the man you loved...*I* wanted to be the one you couldn't stop thinking about!'

The man she loved? For a moment she thought he was talking about himself. 'I lost Joshua a long time ago,' she said slowly. 'I grew and changed but he could never respond to the changes in me. When...when he died I think it was a kind of awful relief... that was what made me feel so guilty when I——'

'When you what?'

When I fell in love with you. 'When we made love.'

'When I seduced you,' he corrected her. 'I knew you'd had a little too much to drink and I took shameless advantage of you.'

Victoria shook her head, her throat tight with fear as she admitted. 'It was me. *I* took advantage of *you*. I knew that if you knew where I had been—at Joshua's funeral—you'd be horrified, disgusted——'

He stepped closer, not touching her except by the warmth of his understanding. 'Horrified, perhaps, but not disgusted. Angry and betrayed, even—I felt all those things later—but that night nothing would have stopped me. I was determined to have you. And I still am...'

'You were disgusted.' She refused to accept his words. 'You looked at me with such contempt——'

Now he touched her. His hand first on the soft shoulder of her dress. 'Do you know what contempt is? It's the feeling of a prudent man for an enemy who is too formidable to be safely opposed. And don't look like that—it wasn't *you* who was the enemy, it was Joshua, safely dead, unreachable, enshrined in perfect memory. How could I compete with that? I wanted to be perfect for you, but I'm not. And nor are you perfect for me.' His hand touched her exposed collarbone, her jaw, her cheek. 'We're too thankfully human for that. I've admired several women for several virtues but none seemed to possess them all... until you. I was wallowing in the ultimate male fantasy—knowledge in the pursuit of innocence. I had this rosy, unrealistic vision of us fitting together like two halves of a whole, but that didn't take account of all the missing pieces of our separate personalities, our secret fears and insecurities, and the sin of my damned pride——'

'But what you said was true,' she insisted flatly. 'I was a coward and dishonest, even with myself. I *did* let David's lie about Joshua stand for mainly selfish reasons, because I liked being treated like a real woman instead

of an untouchable wife. But at the same time I wanted
the safety net of my guilt; I didn't want to get *too* involved with you ... I suppose that makes me a tease.'

'You didn't want to get involved with *any* man,' he
corrected her, secretly enchanted by the notion of her as
a provocative sexual manipulator of his desires. His
finger was now tracing around her trembling mouth.
'You had taken on so many responsibilities so early,
missed so much of being young in your grief ... you just
wanted to cautiously dip a toe into the ocean of experiences that flowed around your quietly remote island ...
You wanted to get a little happiness for yourself ...'

'And instead I got you,' said Victoria in a ruefully
shaky whisper, his understanding wrapping her chilled
heart in delicious warmth.

'Not instead ... never instead, but oh, lady, did you
ever get me!' His voice was as hushed as hers, the dis-
tinctive, smoky blend of undertones smudged by the faint
French burr that shadowed his words when he was at
his most emotional. 'I deserved my come-uppance, you
know. I planned a seduction and when I got exactly what
I wanted I discovered that *I* was the one who had been
seduced, *I* was the one who was helpless. Last time you
were in my arms I told you that I loved you, but you
didn't even acknowledge my gift. Perhaps you weren't
ready to receive it. And instead of telling you that it
made no difference to my feelings I slunk off to lick my
wounded pride——'

'Besides, you had a date waiting for you to pick her
up,' Victoria murmured, turning away from his gentle
finger as she recalled the stabbing jealousy she had felt.

He cupped her jaw and forced her to look at him. 'I
didn't see Nicole that night. I rang and cancelled and
then I went out and drove around, cursing myself for
behaving like a caveman and wondering what to do to
redeem myself. When I came back to throw myself on
your mercy you were gone and I drank myself sick
thinking that you hated me. I would have come over the
next day, but——' He suddenly tensed, looking stricken,
despair flickering across the dark eyes.

'But what?' Victoria felt the turmoil shudder through him.

'But I had one or two experiments I had to check on first,' he gritted slowly, adding quickly, with a dread earnestness, as he saw her blink incredulously as she realised what he was telling her, 'They were *very* important. Months of research depended on the data. I couldn't just leave it; a lot of people depend on my work... I started to run the data through the system and then I noticed it was throwing up this odd variable... I suddenly had this incredible idea...and...oh, *hell*!' His hands dropped to clasp loosely around her waist, his head bowed in helpless frustration.

Victoria had seen enough of him at work to know exactly what had happened. She should have been mortified, but instead she felt a rush of love so powerful that she almost weakened and threw herself into his undeserving arms.

'I see.'

His head jerked up as he drew a steadying breath and tumbled grimly back into the fray. 'No, you don't. It wasn't that I forgot about you. I didn't. I mean, you're in my mind all the time, you're part of me now. It's just that—well, this was something I knew with absolute certainty I *could* fix. I—my work is the one area that I'm safe in... I know what I'm doing every step of the way even if I don't exactly know where I'm going. With you it's chaos... For such a quiet, serene little thing you have this incredible capacity for disrupting my logic circuits. I don't suppose in all this rambling I've remembered to tell you again that I love you?'

'No, you haven't.'

'You see? That was supposed to be my opening line, instead I let myself get distracted by the fact that you look so different...' His hands were stroking restlessly up and down her side. 'Welcome home, Victoria, I missed you. I love you. Will you marry me and live happily ever after with me?'

'There's no such thing as happy ever after,' said Victoria faintly. 'Marriage'. The word conjured up a welter of conflicting feelings. In her wildest dreams she had never let herself go that dangerously far... She leaned away from him, trying to assimilate her whirling thoughts, and his body inevitably followed the sway of hers.

'Stop being evasive.' His words were a murmur away from her mouth. 'You noticed how restrained I'm being, darling. It's killing me to touch you like this and not kiss you, not overwhelm you with my feelings, but I'm doing it. Do you love me?'

'Lucas——'

'Of course you do, otherwise you wouldn't have made such beautiful love with me.' He managed to sound both superbly arrogant and avowedly humble.

'On the day of my husband's funeral.' She probed the painful wound but he didn't flinch.

'At a time when you needed to reach out and be touched by another human being, someone warm and vital and strong, someone you could lean on and lose yourself in. I am very honoured to be that man, Victoria. If I were Joshua I would understand that need.'

'If you were Joshua you'd be dead!' she burst out, trying to tear herself away.

'But I'm not. I'm very much alive!' He refused to let her go, perceiving the truth in her stricken eyes. 'I can't promise I'm not going to die on you, Victoria, but I can promise that I'll never willingly leave you. Don't grieve for me yet. Is that why you won't trust me with your love? Oh, Victoria... use your head if not your heart. It could just as easily have been *you* in that car instead of Joshua. You'll die too, one day, but that still gives me *this* day with you. Would you deny us even that much happiness? To refuse the sweets of life because one day they'll be gone is as senseless as ... as wishing to be born an old woman because one day you're going to grow old!'

Put like that it did sound ridiculous, but the heartaches of the past were a bitter lesson. Victoria pushed against his hard chest and felt the quiver of his heart against her palm.

He put his hand over hers. 'You took your wedding-ring off.'

'What?'

'While you were away you stopped wearing Joshua's ring.' he said huskily. 'That was the second thing I noticed about you today, when I got over my jealousy at wondering why being away from me had made you sexier than ever...'

She flushed as she looked down at their two hands entwined against his chest. At Queenstown she had made a conscious decision to remove that small gold link with Joshua, and thus lay the past to rest. So why was she still letting it control her future. 'Yes...'

'New beginnings...?' he guessed softly.

'I...yes...' Her eyes were bright with her fears and he smiled tenderly.

'With me?'

'I...' She swallowed, her courage wavering. 'Lucas, I've only been a widow for a few weeks. We can't——'

'Fall in love? But we already have. But if it's a proper wooing you want I can arrange it. I won't rush you. Only don't leave me in suspense too long, Victoria. I don't think I'd be very good at unrequited love. I'd probably do something rash and make you hate me.'

'Oh, Lucas, I could never do that.' She felt weak tears sting her eyes.

'No?' His crooked mouth mocked her with its wryness.

'Well, sometimes,' she admitted. 'I—I don't always know myself around you. I do things, I feel things that I—I'm not very comfortable with. You make it all sound so simple, but it's not. There are other people to think of and...I don't know if I'm ready to get married again——'

His whole body tautened as he made a grim decision. If she wasn't receptive to his courtship then maybe blackmail would serve. 'What if you're pregnant?'

Oh, God, he was good. He knew exactly which buttons to push. Victoria's eyes went dark with shocked pleasure at the idea. He smiled bitterly, mistaking her shock.

'I didn't use anything. You might be carrying my child even now. If you're worried about the kind of gossip our marriage might generate, just think of the rabid speculation an illegitimate baby would provoke. That would really ruin your image as the grieving widow!'

'I'm not pregnant,' she said quietly. He swore and she went on steadily, 'But, if I were, I would be proud to have your baby, in or out of wedlock.'

'Then what in the hell are we arguing about?' he yelled in honest confusion. 'You love me, I love you. Believe it or not, it really *is* that simple!'

'If it were that simple we wouldn't *be* arguing,' Victoria pointed out with stubborn logic. 'We only met weeks ago; how can we know if we're compatible?'

'We'll have a long and *very* passionate engagement——'

'I'm not sure what you expect from a wife——'

'To love me and my children——'

'I'd have to let David and the rest of them get used to the idea that you and I——'

'Victoria,' he told her with thorough satisfaction, 'how do you think I explained to your *adult* stepbrood why I wanted to move into their house and pine in wait for you?'

'Oh.'

'Yes. Oh. In fact, if it's David you're most concerned about, and I suspect it is, then I suggest you come with me now and settle this once and for all...'

'I have to unpack——'

'Forget your housewifely obsession for a moment. This is our future at stake!'

His BMW was in the garage around the back. Victoria sensed it would suit his mood to drive like a madman, but after stuffing her unceremoniously into the front passenger seat he drove sedately through the familiar streets to his home, listening to all her protests and only commenting, as he pulled into the driveway, 'I noticed you haven't thrown our differing financial status into your stonewall. At least I know, my unworldly darling, that you're not lusting after me for my money...'

'There's no need to be crude,' protested Victoria as she got out of the car.

'There's every need. Being gentle with you is obviously not working.' Before he opened the front door he stopped and kissed her, long and hard. 'That's to keep us going,' he said in a stifled voice as she tried to get her breath back. 'And to remind you what you're missing by making me go through all this agony.' He kissed her again in the hall, just to make sure she didn't forget and it took a long time for him to decide that her memory was sufficiently reinforced.

Victoria's new finery was thoroughly mussed by the time that they found Scott and David playing chess in the big, comfortable room mockingly referred to by Gabby as the 'playroom'. Gabby herself was lounging on the couch reading a folder with the company logo on the front, but she tossed it aside with delight when she saw the arrivals.

'Victoria! When did you get back? You look fantastic! I love that haircut—makes your eyes look huge!' She didn't mention Victoria's swollen, ravished mouth, probably because she noticed her brother's heavy-lidded expression of sultry warning, but Victoria blushed anyway, murmuring 'hello' through her tingling lips, feeling slightly awkward as she greeted Scott, wondering if he resented her for the way she had returned his generosity in welcoming her into his home.

'It's about time you came back, Victoria,' was all he said, but she noticed the twinkle in his eyes. Of course Lucas would have told him everything, and of course he would be on his stepson's side.

David was a little sheepish in his own greeting, and she soon discovered why. Gabby was sporting a small but exquisite emerald and diamond ring.

'I finally decided that he had potential,' joked the young woman with a glowing look at David. To Victoria's amusement he looked smug rather than irritated by the implication that he was acquiring a managing wife.

Lucas didn't let the distraction work for long. 'Would you mind spreading some of your good fortune around, David? How about telling your stepmother that you won't think she's besmirching the family honour and committing her soul to the fires of hell by agreeing to marry me.'

Victoria was appalled by his blunt approach to such a delicate subject.

Gabby looked shocked, but for all the wrong reasons. 'You didn't tell him that, did you, Victoria?'

'Or words to that effect,' Lucas announced. 'She has this quaint notion that love is no solid basis for marriage.'

David frowned, and looked even more sheepish still. 'If it's because of me, Tory, I told you before you went away that I didn't mean those things I said to you after the funeral. I guess I was just jealous that things seemed to be falling into place so neatly for you when my own life was in such emotional turmoil. I won't say I exactly welcomed Lucas when he moved in, in fact he was a pain in the——' He gave the man a rueful look that told Victoria that neither man had backed away from the confrontation; perhaps they had even enjoyed the outlet for their tempers! 'But you can't say he doesn't have sincere feelings for you... and he's pretty determined——'

'I'll stick like a leech.'

Lucas's whispered vow scalded the back of her neck and Victoria struggled to concentrate as David continued, becoming vaguely pompous as he got fully into his stride, 'We're only concerned because we want you to be happy... and I guess that means doing what feels right to *you*. I know that's what Dad would have wanted... for you to be happy and to be loved for yourself. You don't have to prove how strong and independent you are by struggling on alone, because you already *are* all those things. On the other hand——' He strove for impartiality. Now that he was marrying Gabby his loyalties were obviously strained. 'Don't let Lucas do your thinking for you. He can be very persuasive.

Just because *he's* sure, it doesn't mean you have to be——'

'Hell, West, I thought you said you'd help.' Lucas drew Victoria back against his body in a sharply protective gesture looping his arms around her waist in case she should resist.

'Not at the expense of Victoria's happiness,' David said, obviously beginning to appreciate the novelty of having the upper hand against his brilliant boss and prospective brother-in-law. Victoria thought the situation was developing elements of farce as Scott wheeled himself deftly into the fray.

'I think we're all agreed that Victoria's happiness is of paramount importance here. If you're really not sure about marrying Lucas, my dear, then of course you must have more time to make up your mind, and I have the perfect solution!'

'Oh, good!' dripped Lucas sarcastically, his arms tightening possessively. He had a premonition that he wasn't going to like what was coming. His stepfather's manner was dangerously innocent.

'I've decided that it's time I widened my own horizons a bit,' Scott confirmed his worst suspicions. 'I haven't been out of the country since I had my accident and I have a mind to travel. I've had a chat to a few travel people and if I can arrange a companion to go with me I won't have any problems with airlines or overseas hotels or tour-booking companies. The way I see it is, I need a good six months to see the world properly. Now, if Victoria were to come with me—all expenses paid, of course—she could get a bit of the worldly polish that every modern woman aspires to and at the same time have a chance to contemplate her options away from all the pressures of——'

'No!' Lucas lunged out from behind her and for a moment Victoria thought he was going to actually grab Scott by his shirtfront and shake him out of his chair. 'Six months!' he growled hoarsely. 'What the hell are you trying to do, kill me——?' He broke into a stream of guttural French that from Gabby's shocked fascination was every bit as awful as it sounded.

'Did you really mean that?' Victoria felt obliged to interrupt the staccato bursts firing back and forth before someone was lethally wounded.

Lucas turned on her. 'No, of course he didn't. He was just being a bloody interfering old b——'

'Yes, I did.' Scott performed a cunning manoeuvre around his hostile stepson, narrowly missing his toes. He ignored a snarling expletive and looked up into Victoria's sweetly bewildered face. 'Whether you come with me or I get someone else, I'm still going on this trip. It's been hovering in the back of my mind for a while... why do you think I've been so keen to get my fitness back? Renata and I always planned to have a big trip in our twilight years. Well, that's not going to happen now, but it doesn't have to mean that I give up the whole dream. Want to share it with me, Victoria? Rome, Greece, England... Medieval castles and churches galore...'

Lucas had lapsed into rigid silence, shorn of his easy self-confidence, the rage that had stormed through him at his stepfather's offer dammed up by the cold horror of rejection. It was a tempting opportunity for a woman who had never really known freedom and, given her cultural heritage from her father, how could he blame her for choosing a certain love of history over the uncertainty of love? It wasn't that he couldn't match the offer—she knew he could afford to take her anywhere she wished to go—but there would be strings attached to any offer *he* made. He wasn't going to bargain for her love like a commodity. Unlike her first marriage, he wanted this one to be entirely of her own choosing, her love untainted by guilt or any possibility of future regret.

The room was so quiet that Victoria was sure she could hear her heart beating.

'The whole world at your feet, Victoria,' Scott urged, and it came to her in a blinding flash of relief that she didn't care about the rest of the world. She didn't have to share someone else's dream. She had her own, right here.

'I think I'd rather have Lucas at my side than the world at my feet,' she admitted huskily, startled and relieved to realise it was indeed that simple.

For a moment Lucas stared blankly at her and she went vivid red, her freckles standing out like little exclamation marks of horror as she faced the same small eternity of torment that he had faced moments earlier.

'Me?' he asked stupidly, her brilliant, intuitive genius.

'Don't tell me there's another Lucas I should be proposing to,' she said tremulously, hardly noticing the smug grin with which Scott retired gracefully from the field of battle, chivvying David and Gabby along with him as he wheeled triumphantly off to the kitchen to bully some champagne out of Iris's jealous keeping. 'I rather think that one is as much as I can cope with.'

'You're proposing—to *me*?' The warmth of Lucas's smile was like a fire leaping under his cold, hard, icy expression. The thaw came in a sudden, swooping rush. He swept her close as she nodded.

'I'll never let you forget it, you know that?'

'Yes, I know,' she said ruefully, willingly handing him the hard-earned victory.

She felt rather than saw his smile as he bent his head and brushed his mouth against hers. 'Whenever we have a fight, I'll throw it in your face,' he teased threateningly.

'Whatever happens, it's all my fault,' agreed Victoria blissfully, welcoming the delicious taste and familiar feel of the rising passion in him as he gathered her slowly, sensuously to his heart. Cherished in his arms, Victoria knew that she had chosen the best of all possible worlds. With Lucas love would be the most exhilarating and challenging adventure of her life!

· HARLEQUIN ◆ PRESENTS®

BARBARY WHARF

**Home to the *Sentinel*
Home to passion, heartache and love**

Charlotte Lamb

The **BARBARY WHARF** six-book saga concludes with Book Six, SURRENDER. The turbulent relationship between Nick Caspian and Gina Tyrrell reaches its final crisis. Nick is behaving like a man possessed, and he claims Gina's responsible. She may have declared war on him, but one thing is certain— Nick has never surrendered to anyone in his life and he's not about to start now. Will this final battle bring Nick and Gina together, or will it completely tear them apart?

SURRENDER (Harlequin Presents #1540)
available in March.

October: BESIEGED (#1498)
November: BATTLE FOR POSSESSION (#1509)
December: TOO CLOSE FOR COMFORT (#1513)
January: PLAYING HARD TO GET (#1522)
February: A SWEET ADDICTION (#1530)
If you missed any of the BARBARY WHARF titles, order them by sending your name, address, zip or postal code, along with a check or money order for $2.89 for each book ordered (please do not send cash), plus 75¢ for postage and handling ($1.00 in Canada), for each book ordered, payable to Harlequin Reader Service, to:

In the U.S.	In Canada
3010 Walden Avenue	P.O. Box 609
P.O. Box 1325	Fort Erie, Ontario
Buffalo, NY 14269-1325	L2A 5X3

Please specify book title(s) with your order.
Canadian residents please add applicable federal and provincial taxes.   BARB-M

Where do you find hot Texas nights, smooth Texas charm and dangerously sexy cowboys?

DEEP IN THE HEART

Wedding Bells—Texas Style!

Even a Boston blue blood needs a Texas education. Ranch owner J. T. McKinney is handsome, strong, opinioned and totally charming. And he is determined to marry beautiful Bostonian Cynthia Page. However, the couple soon discovers a Texas cattleman's idea of marriage differs greatly from a New England career woman's!

CRYSTAL CREEK reverberates with the exciting rhythm of Texas. Each story features the rugged individuals who live and love in the Lone Star State. And each one ends with the same invitation...

Y'ALL COME BACK...REAL SOON!

Don't miss *DEEP IN THE HEART* by Barbara Kaye. Available in March wherever Harlequin books are sold.

HARLEQUIN ROMANCE®

**Harlequin Romance
makes love
an adventure!**

Don't miss
next month's
exciting story in

THE BRIDAL COLLECTION

RESCUED BY LOVE
by Anne Marie Duquette

THE BRIDE wanted a new future.
THE GROOM was haunted by his past.
THEIR WEDDING was a Grand affair!

Available this month in
The Bridal Collection:
A BRIDE FOR RANSOM
by Renee Roszel
Harlequin Romance #3251

WED-11

HARLEQUIN®

my **Valentine** *1993*

The most romantic day of the year is here! Escape into the exquisite world of love with MY VALENTINE 1993. What better way to celebrate Valentine's Day than with this very romantic, sensuous collection of four original short stories, written by some of Harlequin's most popular authors.

ANNE STUART
JUDITH ARNOLD
ANNE McALLISTER
LINDA RANDALL WISDOM

THIS VALENTINE'S DAY, DISCOVER ROMANCE WITH MY VALENTINE 1993

Available in February wherever Harlequin Books are sold.   VAL93

Harlequin is proud to present our best authors, their best books and the best for your reading pleasure!

Throughout 1993, Harlequin will bring you exciting books by some of the top names in contemporary romance!

In February,
look for
Twist of Fate by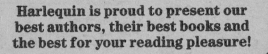

Hannah Jessett had been content with her quiet life. Suddenly she was the center of a corporate battle with wealthy entrepreneur Gideon Cage. Now Hannah must choose between the fame and money an inheritance has brought or a love that may not be as it appears.

Don't miss TWIST OF FATE ...
wherever Harlequin books are sold.

BOB1

ROMANCE IS A YEARLONG EVENT!

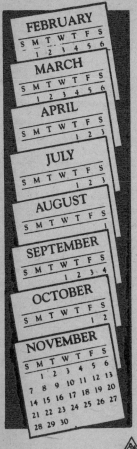

FEBRUARY

S	M	T	W	T	F	S
		1	2	3	4	5	6

MARCH

S	M	T	W	T	F	S
		1	2	3	4	5	6

APRIL

S	M	T	W	T	F	S
					1	2	3

JULY

S	M	T	W	T	F	S
					1	2	3

AUGUST

S	M	T	W	T	F	S
						1

SEPTEMBER

S	M	T	W	T	F	S
			1	2	3	4

OCTOBER

S	M	T	W	T	F	S
					1	2

NOVEMBER

S	M	T	W	T	F	S
	1	2	3	4	5	6
7	8	9	10	11	12	13
14	15	16	17	18	19	20
21	22	23	24	25	26	27
28	29	30				

Celebrate the most romantic day of the year with MY VALENTINE! (February)

CRYSTAL CREEK
When you come for a visit Texas-style, you won't want to leave! (March)

Celebrate the joy, excitement and adjustment that comes with being JUST MARRIED! (April)

Go back in time and discover the West as it was meant to be... UNTAMED—Maverick Hearts! (July)

LINGERING SHADOWS
New York Times bestselling author Penny Jordan brings you her latest blockbuster. Don't miss it! (August)

BACK BY POPULAR DEMAND!!!
Calloway Corners, involving stories of four sisters coping with family, business and romance! (September)

FRIENDS, FAMILIES, LOVERS
Join us for these heartwarming love stories that evoke memories of family and friends. (October)

Capture the magic and romance of Christmas past with HARLEQUIN HISTORICAL CHRISTMAS STORIES! (November)

WATCH FOR FURTHER DETAILS IN ALL HARLEQUIN BOOKS!

CALEND